Voyage to Earth

And Other Stories

More science fiction from mcgrew
Nobots
Mars, Ho!
Yesterday's Tomorrows

Free e-books at mcgrew**books**.com
Hardcover ISBN 978-0-9910531-7-9

Printed in the United States of America

For my fans

Table of Contents

First Contact 1
The Pirate 17
We still haven't found extraforgostnic life 50
Watch your language, young man! 53
Stealth 57
The Naked Truth 65
Cornodium 75
Moroned off Vesta 95
The Exhibit 100
Agoraphobia 106
A Strange Discovery 114
Dumb tourist! 117
The Accidental Traveler 123
Trouble on Ceres 129
Weird Planet 145
Dewey's War 152
Plutus' Revenge 163
Voyage to Earth 168
Sentience 202
Grommler 207
2BR02B 210
The Stories Behind the Stories 218

First Contact

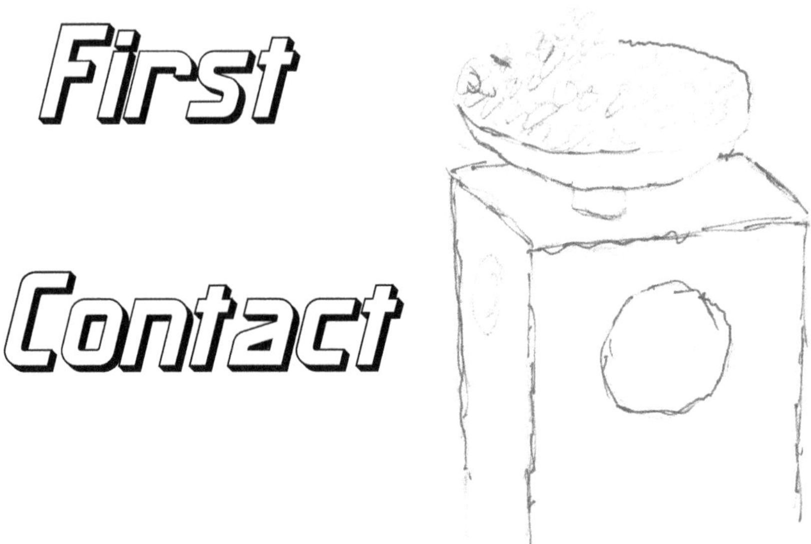

"Damn it, Rick, slow down!"

"Relax, Jack, we can safely cut through an atmosphere at ten times this speed."

"I don't care, we'll look like a shooting star down there, and it's daytime on this side of the planet. We want to be discreet."

"Look, there isn't anything there but plants and animals and rocks and dirt. We saw no lights, no cities, and our telescopes are excellent."

"Still," Jack said, "We don't know for sure. Slow down!"

The green fur on Tubark's neck stood on end as her hairy, tentacled arm with its seven tentacled fingers pointed to the bright afternoon sky. "Do you see that?" she exclaimed. All four of her eyes stared at the sky as her hairy tail drooped and the feathers on her forehead stood up.

"Yes. What was it?"

"I think it is a dragon, as in ancient tales. We think they are only in stories, but maybe dragons are real?"

Targov shook her head. "It cannot be. This must be a dream. Or it is something we know not of. Come, we need to see The Elder."

"Lots of flora and fauna on this planet, Russ, but surveys show no intelligent fauna."

"We're not looking for intelligence, Jack. We're just studying animals. And there seem to be a lot of different species of beast here. We hit the jackpot!"

"But are any sentient?"

"Who cares?"

"I do," Jack replied. "We've never found a sentient species, why haven't we?"

"How should I know? They've wondered that forever! But if there is a sapient species here, they must not be past the hunter-gatherer phase, certainly before discovering electricity. We saw no evidence of civilization from space. No cities or anything like that, no lights. But it is odd that out of all the planets we've explored, of all the alien life we've found, we've never found a sentient animal."

"You think we're the only sentience in the universe? That can't be!"

"Why not? Maybe we are, or maybe we just haven't found any sentience." Russ chuckled. "Maybe they're all so far beyond us that they have invisibility or something. Maybe they all hide!"

The Elder frowned; or what passed as a frown with his species. "Dragons are not real. They are made-up stories, stories to make you deny the maker of the world. They are lies." He twitched his hairy tail and frowned more deeply, all four eyes glaring and the feathers on his forehead standing straight up.

"Well, I do not know what we saw, but we saw *something* with fire come down from the sky. Toward the sunset, away from the water, toward the barren land. We want to look and find out what it is."

The Elder, who didn't look old, scratched his head. "No," he said. "Not alone. There are deadly animals and other dangers. I will send spearmen and clubmen with you for safeness."

He grinned; or at least, the way his eyes moved was the equivalent of a grin. "Maybe it is the maker, come to visit his creation? Or maybe it was a trick of the light. We shall see."

"Hey, Marge, we caught one! Have a look!" Russ was excited. He'd found something like a bat or a bird, but it looked on the video they'd captured that the animal was neither bird nor mammal, or maybe both; it had fur on its body and feathered wings. It was a red animal, about half a meter long. It stood on the ground, wings folded behind it, with two four-taloned bird-like feet on the ground, and strange, tentacle-like arms and fingers collecting its food and sticking it in what passed as its toothy mouth.

"Whoa! Russ, you'd better be recording." Russ glared at her a second, and started laughing. Of course it was being recorded, inside and out, with technology far beyond an MRI or CT scan.

Something rustled in the foliage behind the animal and it jumped up, startled, and flew away. Another animal lumbered out on four legs, with the strange, tentacled arms they had seen on the bat-like creature. It started eating the fruit the flying animal had been dining on.

It whirled around, snarling, and a tentacle swiftly snaked out, grabbed it, and it disappeared into the underbrush.

"I want pictures of whatever grabbed the second specimen. Jackpot, indeed! I wonder how many new species we'll catalog?"

"Don't know," Marge said. "Did your notice that both of those animals were so much alike, but different? Both with feathers and hair, each with four eyes, and each with six limbs, although one had two feet and two wings, and one had four feet, both animals with those prehensile snake-like arms and fingers? The feet were different... a few other things."

"Well, it seems so, but with only two specimens... we saw nothing smaller than that bird-bat, for instance."

"I am curious, myself," the Elder said. "Tubark and Targov will go, since they saw it fall and know where. Katak will record pictures with animal skin and charcoal, Moadir the scribe will record events with writing, and Abat and his crew of spearmen and clubmen will hunt meat and protect from dangerous animals.

"And I will go also."

Abat was taken aback. "Elder? You will go?"

The Elder frowned. "You cannot protect?"

"Yes, but... why?"

"I am an herbmaster and plantmaster. There is poison, and other hidden danger you may not see, hear, or smell. I know all of the lore. I will not lose a party as the Previous did!

"How are the robots holding up, Rick?"

Rick snorted. "Like brand new. None have caught anything since Russ' robot caught those three. Or two and a half or something, Russ says there's not much data from the third. I'm bored."

Jack shrugged. "You should have studied biology instead of engineering. Russ, Marge, and I are all working our butts off. There's tons of data to study. But I worry that we may affect the environment, and thereby affect the ecosystem's evolution. XZ-287 haunts me."

"Jack, you had nothing to do with that planet, or that expedition."

"No, I didn't. But I'm terrified of repeating it. Rick, every species on that planet became extinct! That world was alive and thriving, now it's completely dead and lifeless."

"Well, there were and awful lot of..."

"Unintended consequences. The butterfly effect."

Rick snorted. "I don't worry about butterflies, I worry about dragons."

"Dragons?"

"Yeah, I worry that your butterflies will drag on and on and bore me to death! Stop worrying, we take precautions."

"Yes, but are they enough?"

The party halted at the Elder's insistence. "I smell preyberries," he said.

"Preyberries?" Abat asked. "What are they?"

"You do smell that, do you not? That sweet smell?"

"Yes, it makes me hungry."

"That is preyberries. The gongarath eats them not, but eats those that do. We shall not go farther. Yet. We shall wait until the gongarath has his dinner, then hurry past. You do not want to smell of preyberries, or of anything that eats them!"

They melted into the underbrush on the other side of the trail from the preyberries.

"Where's Marge? She's late for her shift and I'm starving," Russ whined. "Oh, wow! Guys, we got another one." Everyone looked at the largest holographic screen, showing the happenings transmitted by the robot.

An animal that vaguely resembled a small polar bear, except it was covered in sky blue feathers rather than white fur, had those furry tentacled arms, and a face that looked nothing like a bear's, looked around with its four eyes.

"It didn't take the bait," Rick said dumbly.

Russ looked at him. "Well, no kiddin'. But why?"

"Watch and see, I'm curious," Jack said. Just then, Margaret came in.

"Sorry I'm late, Russ, I overslept." Her hair indeed looked unbrushed.

"Your loss, Marge. Check out the screen! We got another one," he said, seeming to forget all about his earlier starvation.

The animal sniffed around the robot that held its large tray of preyberries. It lost interest, and went over next to a bluefeather bush and seemed to roll itself into a feathery ball that looked like all the other bluefeather bushes.

"Whoa!" Margaret said. "That was different!"

Jack laughed. "It's all different. We can probably forget everything we learned in all our biology classes here, that only applies to Earth life. Even the chemistry is different. We'll see all kinds of other stuff even weirder, I'll bet."

"I wonder if all the bluefeathers they cataloged by telescope were the flora and which were those weird blue bears?" Margaret mused, as another of the bat-birds landed, and took a single piece of fruit before being startled and dropping it and flying away.

A different, smaller four-eyed species waddled up on its four legs and started feasting on the preyberries, again grasping them with those strange multi-tentacled limbs all these animals seemed to have.

The gongarath hadn't gone far, and had been lying in wait. A tentacle sprang out, grabbing the unknowing animal. A clawed foot whipped forth from the faux bluefeather bush and grabbed the tentacle, which dropped the animal and went limp. The animal scurried off, and the faux bluefeather uncurled and began dining on the gongarath.

"Wow," Margaret said.

"Still hungry, Russ?" Jack asked, grinning.

The Elder was very pleased. "We can continue," he told his people. "Our spiritual friend, the bushbeast, has vanquished our foe for us. But do not eat the fruit. Only those who smell of the fruit will the gongarath devour. Do not even touch it, or its juice!"

By then the animals had worn a path from the trail to the bait robot, its camouflage partly torn away by the animals. The Elder spied the robot at the same time as Tubark. "What is that thing, Elder?" she asked.

He frowned. "It is not in the lore, and I have studied it all. Katak! I need a record!"

"Holy crap! Did you see that?" Jack said rather loudly.

"See what?" Margaret asked.

"Clubs and spears. I think we may have found sentience! Hey, Russ! Somebody wake Rick up!"

"Now, hold on," Russ replied. "That doesn't prove sentience. Heck, back on Earth crows use tools, but it doesn't make them sentient. Let him sleep. He's an engineer, not a biologist. Wake him up if something breaks."

"But he shouldn't have come down so damned fast! I tried to warn him when we were landing. They might have seen us."

"Relax, what could happen? We were just a shooting star.

The Elder became cautious. "Be careful," he said. "It will be starting to get dark soon. Stay to the left and touch nothing orange. Orange is death. It is poison. Walk single file. To touch that orange is death." Right then, one of the clubmen screamed.

"I spoke too late," the Elder said, and dug in his bag for a certain herb. "But perhaps not too late. If I can draw out the poison he will live." He attended to his wounded charge.

A while later as the sun was setting, the clubman awoke.

"What is your name, clubman?"

"Ragar, Elder."

The Elder was relieved. "You will not perish tonight, Ragar. If you knew not your name, you would be dead by morning, but the herbs have power and we were swift. How do you feel?"

"Weak and shaky. I feel thorns all over and my mind and senses are dulled."

"We shall rest a while longer, then. You are very lucky, Ragar. Orange is death out here. Do not touch the orange again! It is poison. The second time you touch the orange there is nothing anyone can do for you. Death will be swift and terrible."

"Elder..."

"Yes?"

"How did I get here? I do not even remember being called to duty today."

Two of the Elder's eyes twirled in mirth. "Never you will. And you are lucky it is so, for you would not want to remember the horrible pain."

He turned and faced his troupe. "He shall live," the Elder informed them. "But we must make a litter or he cannot travel. It looks like we rest here this night to avoid that. Travel will be slower now, as he will be weak."

Rick threw his book on the floor in frustration. "To hell with this," he said aloud to no one, since no one was there. "I'm an explorer, damn it. I'm not sitting in this can the whole expedition, I'm exploring."

He went to the supply room, half empty now since the robots were no longer in storage. "Damn," he said to himself. "The sun won't be up for another hour." He started donning the environment suit.

The three scientists were sitting down for breakfast, and Russ asked "Where's Rick?"

"Don't know," Margaret mumbled through a mouthful of food. "Something important probably broke."

"Yeah," Jack answered. "His brain. A long time ago." Both of the other scientists laughed.

"Pass the salt, would you?" Russ asked, and sipped his coffee and made a face. "Cold," he said, and put his cup in the microwave, which failed to start. He pulled out his phone and tried to call Rick, to no avail; the phone informed him that there was no signal coming from Rick's phone. He fumed. "Damn him! Why is his phone off? The damned microwave is busted. What good is an engineer if he's never available?

"Hey, Marge, did Rick ever show up for breakfast?"

"I don't know. Jack?"

"Nope, haven't seen him all morning."

"Crap. Well, my coffee's cold. Guess I'll have to make a new pot."

"Has anyone checked his room?" Margaret queried.

"Well," Russ replied, "I guess I'll check his quarters... after I get another cup of coffee!"

But Rick wasn't in his quarters. After he made more coffee and drank a cup, Russ looked. There was no Rick. He called Margaret. "Rick's not in his room. We need to search the ship, he might have had some sort of medical incident. He could be in trouble."

Fifteen minutes later, Margaret discovered that one of the environment suits was missing. She got on the phone after setting it to ship-wide. "We're in trouble, guys. That damned fool Rick went outside. Meet me at the airlock and we'll figure out what to do."

"We?" Russ thought. "She's heading this disaster. Damn that assbasket Richard!"

He thought a few other things that were far worse.

"How is he, Elder?"

"He will live, but will never again be a clubman. He will be far too weak for physical work for the rest of his days. But he can walk now, the sun is ready to rise and the sky is lighter, so we shall continue. We are almost at the barren land. Have we meat?

"Much, Elder. Too much."

"Too much does not exist."

After standing in the airlock while ultraviolet light sanitized the suit, Rick had strolled outside, feeling invincible in his environment suit and forgetting everything that had been drilled into him about this mission—leave no trace you were ever there. Take nothing but records, and leave nothing, not even footprints. You do not want to be the unwitting cause of a catastrophe.

He walked through the barrens and into the life, with all its varied children, many of them deadly.

He had no knowledge that orange was death.

Possibly for the entire crew. After strolling for an hour he returned, and entered the ship at the same time the natives were entering the barrens.

"The dangers I know are passed," the Elder said. "Dangers I know not are future. All must be wary. We are but babes."

"What is that thing in the distance, Elder?" Abat asked.

The Elder frowned at him. "Which of my words do you not understand? I know not what is ahead. It is a strange thing, an alien thing. It is not in the lore."

"Where in the *hell* have you been, you son of a..."

"Shut up, Russ, I'm in charge. Where the hell *have* you been, idiot? Why in the hell..."

Rick had his helmet off and was starting to remove the gloves, the bottom of his suit stained orange from something he had brushed against. He shrugged and interrupted. "I went for a walk. Is that a crime?"

Russ glowered silently, looking like he was going to tear the engineer's head off, perhaps with his teeth.

"Yes, it is, moron," Jack replied. "Especially if you've killed this planet. You have heard of XZ-287?"

"Hey, I was wearing a..." He screamed and collapsed.

“Oh, crap!” Jack swore mildly. “Heart trouble?” He rolled him over. Rick stared, eyes darting wildly.

“What the...” Jack started, before grimacing in mortal pain and collapsing himself.

They stood maybe ten meters from the ship, in awe of the huge thing. Katak stood for a minute, then got busy with his charcoal.

“Elder?” inquired Tubark.

The Elder smiled, a peculiar movement of the four eyes. “Well, it is most certainly not a dragon. But what it is? All stay, I will investigate.”

He strode forward, and when he got closer, the giant thing startled him and shocked him deeply. A pocket door slid open revealing a closet sized space, and there were lights inside! The only lights he had ever seen in his life were in the sky, besides lamps with flame, and these were not flame. And how can an opening in a mountain appear like that? He walked inside to examine it, especially curious of he cool lighting, not like fire at all, and the door slid closed again.

Everyone was in a panic. The Elder was missing inside that shiny mountain, and there were frantic poundings as if he were trying to kick his way out.

The Elder was in even more of a panic than his charges, until the airlock’s interior door opened and he saw the strange creatures unconscious and dying on the ground.

This was beyond belief. What were those things? But he would help them if he could, as he would with any stricken animal. He got his herbs and neutralized the poisons. But now what? How could he get out of this mountain he had trapped himself in?

He huddled by where the opening he had come in had been. Maybe it would open again.

The next to last to be exposed, Margaret came to first. She was on pins and needles, electric currents all over her body, and her mind was nearly useless. She wondered where she was and how she got there?

She sat up, vision blurred and a roar and whistle in her ears. And she was so weak! Her vision and hearing improved after a couple of minutes, and she saw Russ starting to twitch, then noticed the animal by the door. Where was she? She tried vainly to remember. She *did* remember the trip here, and the landing, but the memory of the landing was very hazy.

She opened the airlock, hoping the strange beast would go in. It did. She closed the inside door, and the outside door opened after the ultraviolet did its work.

Russ was sitting up, blinking. Jack was twitching. Rick was still. She went over to him and felt for a pulse.

The pulse was very weak, and he was as pale as death.

"Elder! You are alive! Thank the Maker! Are you all right?" Abat asked worriedly.

"Yes. Bewildered, but physically sound."

"What was there?"

The Elder ignored him. "Moadir!" he called. "Your service is needed."

"Yes, Elder. What do you wish me to record?"

The Elder looked at Abat with three eyes and Moadir with one. "I saw light inside the small cave in the shiny mountain. When I went in to investigate, I was trapped inside. It is not good to be trapped like that, hard it is to not panic.

"But the inside opened into a large cavern, and I saw strange creatures collapsed on the cave's ground. I saw orange on one and knew it was the death.

"I have never seen any creatures as such, nor heard of them in the lore. These beasts were nothing like I have seen in the world. They had only two legs and only two eyes, and their arms were very strange as well; stiff, not limber like ours. They had their bodies covered with something, I know not what or why. But as any good herbmaster, I made the poison not poison.

"Eventually, after one of the strange animals awoke, the wall opened to the small chamber. Hoping I could get out, I went in, and the wall closed up and trapped me again. Then the other wall opened and I was free.

"I have never seen such so strange. I can describe nothing inside the mountain, there are no words. I must think much on this. But we have surely found Tubark's and Targov's 'dragon'.

"We will now head back to home. I think we may learn nothing more here, and my soul tells me this is a very dangerous place.

"This lore will be talked about for generations!"

The three of them sat at a table trying to figure out what to do next. Rick had awakened last, didn't know who he was, and died a few hours later. His body was in the freezer. With no engineer they would have to call the expedition off and go home. "Besides," Jack said, "I don't know how you two fared, but my brain's not functioning normally and I can barely lift this, uh, this... this coffee cup. Perhaps we can collect the robots without, uh, um, Rick."

"Maybe," Marge said doubtfully. "We certainly can't leave them here."

Jack shivered. "XZ-287."

Marge shuddered and Russ shook. Marge said "Yes. And I don't know about you two, but I think my IQ has dropped, uh, severely. I feel drugged. I'm really afraid we'll mess something up terribly. XZ-287 haunts me, too. Russ, are you up to collecting the, uh... the robots?"

"I don't know, I feel drugged and stupid, too. I'll try."

The robots were collected, leaving no trace. But they lost a lot of data; Russ was not only not an engineer, his thought processes were terribly disrupted. He felt like he hadn't slept in days.

The sentient group's evidence was among the lost data.

Fortunately, the ship was simple to operate. After one told it the destination, it could pilot itself. After the robots were collected and other preliminaries necessary, it rose slowly.

"Elder, Look!" Abat exclaimed anxiously, pointing. They were barely out of the barrens, and had seen some strange objects... animals? ...floating to the mountain. Katak drew furiously, as he had done when the strange floating things, one of which they had seen on the trip to the barrens, had floated past.

It was the Earthian ship on its way home, rising into the sky, but there was no way he could know that. A council of Elders he would have to call. Surely with the combined wisdom and knowledge of all the Elders they could figure this out.

"There are trace amounts of a type of molecule we haven't seen before, Doctor Rhome, but it seems to be an incredibly strong neurotoxin."

Russ nodded. "That makes sense; I still feel drugged."

"There was a different alien molecule as well that seems to bind with the neurotoxin, neutralizing it and allowing it to be excreted with urination. We were able to synthesize it after some study. Apply this cream to your temples and the back of your neck every morning for a week, and come back for another examination. I've already given Dr. Niven medication, and Dr. Tyson has an appointment this afternoon. None of you know where the substance came from?"

"Rick was wearing part of an environment suit when we came to. He must have gone outside, despite everyone's warnings."

"Well, at any rate you should feel much better in a week, and by month's end you should almost be back to normal. But I doubt if any of your lost memory will be restored. We'll have to see about that."

"Thank you, Doctor."

"See the receptionist for that appointment on your way out."

The Elder spoke to his fellow Elders on the council. "This was indeed a puzzling encounter. You have all read Moadir's record and seen the drawings of Katak. What say you of all of this strangeness?"

Elder Golblath spoke. "Elder Varchov, like you I know not what to think. This sounds like magic."

"There is no magic. Magicians are tricksters!" Elder Groll replied.

"That is what I mean. Magic is anything you do not understand, and this we understand not at all."

Elder Nilbud spoke. "According to Elder Varchov and his people, there were heavy things floating in air like feathers, even the huge shiny mountain, there was cold fire, and more. Say I that if anyone should see this again, that we hide from them. There could be more peril than any have ever seen."

The Elders took a vote. The result was unanimous. "It is agreed then. If such should happen again, wisdom says we should hide."

Two years later the same crew was back, with a different engineer, who had been cautioned by Jack to descend slowly. There would be no shooting stars this time.

But the natives had been watching the barrens closely ever since their first visit, and stayed put until the aliens left.

Their data collected and specimens studied, they were on their way back to Earth once again.

"Very good expedition, Marge," said Russ.

"Yes, we did learn a lot about this planet," she replied. "Five hundred fauna species, twice as many flora. And from only fifteen robots!"

Jack mused. "I wonder why we've never found any sentient species anywhere? Something told me we'd find it here, I was sure there would be sentience here, but I don't know why I was so sure."

Russ grinned. "Maybe they're all so far beyond us that they have invisibility or something. Maybe they all hide!"

The Pirate

Bobby Washington was excited and could hardly wait; he hadn't been in a fight since he had left prison, and now he had a chance.

Bobby loved to fight. Even though he couldn't see the lightning flash that was attempting to disable electronics or the green beam that was burning a hole in the fleeing transport, he knew that this was going to be fun.

It was his first raiding party as a pirate.

He hoped the transport's captain was a woman. Even more fun!

He was, of course, by no means a good man. Born thirty years earlier in the south side of Chicago in the ancient Mercy Hospital, he was addicted to opioids when he was born; his mother was an addicted prostitute. He had no idea who his father was, and neither did his mother.

He last saw her when he was five, when the state put him in foster care because his mother neglected him. Heroin does that to a person, and modern opioids were far worse. She was murdered when he was nine, and he didn't hear about it for a year.

Jose Ramos, the son of immigrants to the US from Mexico, was born on the same day in the same hospital. His parents spoke Spanish at home, and Jose didn't learn English until he started school, where he learned to speak the language. His father Esteban was a cook at a small bar and grill, and his mother Juanita was a clerk in a convenience store. As hard working as they were, they were still very poor; cooks and clerks earned little, since their jobs mostly boiled down to making sure the computers and robots didn't go crazy, and one could easily make do without money in society. Most people had no jobs at all. Few jobs paid much unless they required higher education.

Jose dreamed of being a space Marine as he grew up. His favorite pastime was reading about historical military campaigns, even if they were dry, boring ones like the ancient and to his modern eyes, nearly unreadable *We Were Soldiers, and Young.* He, of course, had the same problem reading that twentieth century book as someone from the twentieth century would have had reading Shakespeare. He enjoyed fictional war stories as well, more than the nonfiction. But he could learn more from nonfiction.

When he wasn't reading books and watching videos about war, he played laser tag with his buddies. That was one game that someone had to have money for, since you can't print out a laser. His parents had bought one second-hand for his Christmas present one year. It was his most treasured possession.

By our twenty first century standards his family was very well off, having everything they needed and most of what they wished for. In his time, he was considered poor, as were ninety nine percent of the population.

All in all, Jose was a pretty lucky kid, even if his parents got almost all of their food from government handouts.

Bobby was certainly not a lucky kid. He bounced from foster home to foster home, often abused, often hungry, sometimes molested.

He was a terrible student in school. Barely literate and numerate, he hated to read, to do math, to learn anything but how to get away with stealing and how to win fights.

One day he was sitting in homeroom in his freshman year of high school, bored out of his mind as usual, when the teacher announced "Today we have a very special guest. Everyone in the school is to go to the gymnasium to meet him."

The class followed her to the gym, which was seldom used for anything and never as a gym, since the floor was in such disrepair.

When all of the students were assembled, the principal announced "Meet Mister Dewey Green, one of the Green-Osbourne Transport System's founders and the CEO of that company!"

Half of the assembly gave him half-hearted applause. Bobby sat on the bleacher, head resting on one hand and the other hand doodling as he pretended to take notes.

"Good morning, students. I'm here to talk about the value of a good education," Mister Green started.

Bobby ignored him.

Jose was attending the same school, and also ignored him, instead talking to a disinterested girl about his love for all things military. His parents were readers, and he had inherited their love of books and education as most readers' children do. An excellent student and very qualified candidate for a higher education, he had his mind set on the military instead. He intended to enlist in the North American Space Marine Corps as soon as he was old enough, right after graduating high school.

The shipping executive began speaking. "Now, I have no idea what it's like to be in your shoes," he said, looking over the poverty-stricken students in this dilapidated south side school. He couldn't help noticing the water dripping from various places in the ceiling, the ruined hardwood floor, and wondered why society accepted such a thing. "But I can tell you this, you can escape it. But you have to study hard and stay out of trouble.

"I wasn't born wealthy, kids. I wasn't poor; my parents owned a grocery store and a restaurant. My mom wanted me to become a chef!"

He paused for laughter, but none was forthcoming.

"I studied hard, and went on to study electrical engineering after high school. I got a job as an engineer at

Orion Transport, and while working there went on to earn my Master's Degree.

"My partner, Charles Osbourne, was a friend since junior high, and after he got his mechanical engineering degree we went way in debt to buy two beat up, unsalvageable wrecks and used the parts from both to build a new kind of transport vessel. We thought it was the best there was, and I still think it was the best of its time.

"We weren't poor by any means, but we lived like we were to make sure we could afford the venture, as well as taking business classes. Charles and I both now have MBAs. Eventually we'd built the best and biggest shipping company in the solar system.

"Now, I doubt any of you could manage that, there's a thing called 'middle class privilege', but if you work hard, your children might!

"I'm here to announce that our company is going to actively recruit graduates from this school and schools like it, kids like you who start life without any advantages at all. We'll be hiring and training ship's captains, clerks, maintenance workers, and many other positions. Yes, you no longer need a college degree to pilot a ship.

"It isn't going to be easy. You need to maintain at least a C average in your grades, with none failing and no more than two Ds. And if you get arrested, you're out of luck as far as we're concerned. We don't hire criminals, and few other companies will hire you if you have a criminal record, either.

"So stay out of jail. If you ever get convicted of a felony, your life's pretty much ruined. You're going to be living in government housing, printing everything out, and eating from the government food pantries. I'm sure more than a few of you know about them."

Of course, all of them were already using them.

He continued talking for quite some time. Jose wasn't interested; he was going to be a space marine, and instead was boring the annoyed girl next to him who was trying to listen to the shipping magnate.

Bobby wasn't interested, either. He was going to make angel tears and sell them to hookers and other addicts. Neither one heard a word of what G-O's CEO had uttered.

Since one doesn't learn right from wrong in school, Bobby had no one to teach him. He was in the "new" two hundred year old Joliet prison by the time he was sixteen, tried as an adult and convicted of armed robbery. It was the first place he'd ever lived that wasn't infested with roaches. Of course he never noticed the prison's quaint architecture, it having been built two hundred years earlier.

Jose, as expected, joined the space marines after graduation. His experience was all in low Earth orbit where Earth's various governments and the United Nations had authority. None of its governments had much to do with anything past the moon, except to collect taxes from the spacers living in the huge habitat domes in the asteroid belt and on Mars and Titan, and pass stupid laws that made sense on Earth but no sense at all in space.

He had collected several combat medals and reached the rank of sergeant, and was just about to re-enlist after his four year hitch when he heard about deep space soldiering. The Green-Osbourne Transportation Company was recruiting for positions in a deep space security fleet. He signed the discharge papers and headed to the GOTS recruitment office, where he handed in an application and résumé.

His interview was two days later. "It says here, Mr. Ramos, that you were in the marines."

"Yes, sir. Space duty. Earned a few medals and advanced fast."

"Huh. Low Earth orbit."

"That's where the pirates were then, sir. Our military was protecting our country's commercial interests."

"But no interplanetary experience."

"No, sir. Combat experience. Nobody's done combat outside low Earth orbit. The man you're looking for doesn't exist."

"Well," the executive said with a smile, "I think he does. You've fought pirates for the last few years. I think you're our man, Mister Ramos."

"Thank you, sir," Jose said with a big grin.

"Oh, and by the way," the shipper said, shaking Ramos' hand, "You're now commander."

"Sir?"

"You have the experience and we'll supply the necessary leadership education and teach you about the ships and their workings. You've already held leadership positions, and we intend to send you to Annapolis. You've seen combat. You're perfect, Commander Ramos."

"Wow, that's a lot higher rank than when I was in the service!" Indeed, he was an enlisted man being given a commission in GOTS' private army, going from E-5 to O-5; GOTS used naval rankings in its fleet.

"Well, consider it a promotion, then. At any rate, you're to go to Mars with Green-Osbourne's new defense force, and you're in command. Earth's governments have pretty much stopped Earthian space piracy, but we companies shipping to distant bodies are on our own. Piracy around Mars has gotten way too far out of hand."

Asteroid mining was small-time until two centuries earlier when a new material was discovered on Ceres. It was a type of rare earth that was capable of being magnetized a hundred times stronger than twenty first century ferromagnetic materials. Motors made with these new materials were incredibly efficient; a one by two meter solar panel on the roof of an automobile was sufficient to run the car on a cloudy day. Of course, solar panel technology was far, far better than in solar's twentieth century beginnings, and of course batteries were necessary at night, and especially in freezing weather. Battery technology, too, had advanced greatly.

Earth's governments had another space race when these materials were discovered, with domed cities being built on the planet Mars, the dwarf planet Ceres, and the protoplanet Vesta, and a few of the larger asteroids that were composed of useful materials.

Mars' gravity was perfect for manufacturing magnets, even better than the microgravity of space. The Europeans and Australians jumped on it, with Europe building mining stations on Ceres and Titan and the Australians building Martian smelting facilities, and the North Americans building robot factories and agricultural farms, all inside the gigantic Martian domes.

United Nations treaties between various governments kept armed government vessels no farther from Earth than the moon, as had existed (some said mysteriously) for centuries, and later the UN became a world government. Politics makes strange bedfellows, and as a result of history, space piracy flourished in deep space after being almost completely eliminated near Earth.

The GOTS warships were legal, since Green-Osbourne Transportation Systems wasn't a government. The ships were brand new and still being delivered, and Ramos and the company's human resource arm would have to find and train people to man the ships.

Soldiers to man the ships, even though half of the soldiers manning the ships were women. They all needed training, including Jose, who had never flown on a deep space flight before.

It took a full year for the battleships in Mars' orbit to be finished, and crews trained to fly them. Jose alternated between teaching martial arts and learning how the interplanetary craft worked. Training was at the Annapolis

Mars dome, which had originally been settled from the US state of Maryland.

The company president, Charles Osbourne, accompanied the lead ship's shakedown cruise, taking notes. Now that the ships were operational and tested, crews would have to be trained in space combat.

"Excuse me, sir," Commander Ramos said to President Osbourne, "I'd like to suggest that we hire more military veterans. It would save a lot of time and training."

"Well, I'll take that under advisement, Mr. Ramos. But I want our force to be better than any Earthian army."

A year later it was, and Green-Osbourne already had far better ships and armament than any army on Earth, and far, far better than any other shippers.

Dewey's army, now armed and trained, stayed in orbit around Mars when there was no inbound or outbound traffic. As of yet the defense fleet was only ten ships, protecting dozens of transports, not counting other companies' transports. G-O protected its competitors' ships as well, as they certainly didn't want pirates to have more ships, but of course the priority was GOTS transports.

"Mayday! Mayday! Seven bogeys coming in fast!"

Commander Ramos checked his instruments. He would have a fix on the nearly invisible freighter coming in and decelerating, and radar and radio transmission fixes on the "bogeys," the thieves who would plunder the freight carrier. The brigands were about twenty minutes from the transport, and the soonest his ten ship fleet could get there was half an hour.

"How well are you armed?" the commander asked, knowing that his fleet would show up in the middle of a fight.

"Two atomics, but the way they're coming in an atomic would only destroy one. Ten EMP missiles, and I'm afraid I'm lousy with those things. Plenty of rail slugs and the lasers are good, but I'm not a great shot with those, either."

Jose shook his head sadly. Captain Wallace was on his own for the next half hour, really on his own. Cargo transports seldom carried anyone but the captain unless the cargo was human.

He looked up Captain Wallace's ship; an older model. Setting an EMP off close to his ship would disable it, so he couldn't simply let the pirates get close and set the electromagnetic charge off.

Until he got there.

"Lock it up, Captain," the commander said. "Every damned door. When they try to get in, set off the EMP and we'll take care of it."

"I'll lose propulsion and life support!"

"We'll be there before the air gets too thin or cold and it will slow them down. Use your atomics when the time is right."

"Mayday! Mayday! Four bogies coming in fast!"

Damn, two at once? He sent four ships to help Captain... he looked at his computers... Reynolds. New ship, he should be okay. Especially with half of his fleet getting there in twenty minutes. He wished for more ships. He planned on asking for some when he next saw Mr. Osbourne, and also to see if the engineers could come up with something to make targeting easier for captains inexperienced in combat. Better training as well; it was apparent to Ramos that Wallace wasn't just green, he was brand new. Experienced transport pilots had learned to fight.

Captains' training should include a lot more combat simulation, he was sure.

Jack was terrified. It was his first encounter with pirates, and he had never actually used any of the ship's weaponry, and had only experienced computer controlled simulations. It was only his fourth professional flight.

Four of the pirate ships were close, and the young man was shaking too badly to hit any of them with a rail gun slug, or even hold a laser on one long enough to drill a hole. In a panic, he was too full of fear to think of letting the computers do the targeting. Ramos was right; these fellows needed more training.

The other three murderous ships were holding back.

He dropped an atomic, which only destroyed one ship. The pirates were firing lasers at him, and he was glad he wasn't running any other company's boat, or he'd already be dead. Not a religious man, he prayed none the less.

His screen showed another flash, not nearly as bright as the atomic explosion—a lucky rail gun shot had caused one of the marauding craft to explode. There were five privateer vessels left, and he wondered how many freebooters were on each vessel. Not that it mattered, he was a dead man, he was sure.

One of them managed to get hold of his docking port, and he set off an EMP. The lights and computers and engines all stopped. It was pitch dark and deadly silent; he could hear his own heart pounding.

It was only a few minutes later when Commander Ramos arrived. It took minutes more to attach the warship to the pirate ship and drill out a hatchway. A smokeflasher was thrown in, and his crew, outfitted with night vision glasses and body armor, both physical and electronic, could see through the smoke while pirates couldn't. Even though the EMP had knocked the lights out, the pirates could have antique-style lights with filament bulbs and carbon batteries, or even candles, that an EMP wouldn't disable. Capturing most of them was easy. Killing the ones who fought back was even easier.

"GOTS security!" Commander Ramos yelled when his contingent entered the cargo ship after subduing the men on the pirate ship.

A green laser beam streaked through the door; pirates had gotten in. He worried about the ship's captain, since the only communication was between his crewpeople; all other electronics had been destroyed by the electromagnetic pulse its captain had loosed. His ship and three of the five remaining ships were disabled, and the rest of Ramos' contingent went after the pirates whose boats hadn't been crippled. This was turning out to be a good day; eleven fewer pirate ships and nine fees for the company from the pirate transports' rightful owners.

There were only two plunderers in the transport, and were easily taken out of action. One would need medical treatment, as did another surviving robber on one of the other boats.

Captain Wallace was locked in his pilot room, shaking in fear. The commander drilled a small hole in the door. "Captain Wallace? GOTS security, are you okay?"

"Thank God!" a voice coming dimly through the hole exclaimed before the door opened and the man emerged.

"Lets get you on the boat before it starts getting cold in here. We'll stick around until the tow tug gets here and you can ride back to Mars on her. Oh, and Captain—you should have asked for identification," he said, holding out his phone. "We could have been the pirates trying to trick you."

"Damn," he replied, "You're right. That was stupid of me."

As close as they were to Mars, it didn't take long at all for the tugboat to arrive.

Bobby Washington was introduced to a life of piracy while in prison, when he met Charles Hunter. "Chuckie", as his friends and associates called him, was head of a large pirate gang, and boasted of possessing twenty space ships. "And Bobby," Chuckie said, "I'll get twenty more when I get out of this place. You're paroled next week, right?"

"Yeah. Don't know what I'll do. Probably be back here in two weeks!"

"No you won't. See Ron Cheney, he'll pick you up at the gate when they let you out. I've seen you fight, we could use you."

Cheney was indeed waiting for him when he was paroled. Bobby stuck out his hand, and Cheney ignored it, saying only "get in the car."

He got in. "Where are we going?"

"The belt."

"The what? You mean Washington, DC?"

"Asteroid belt."

This puzzled Washington, who had heard that all the piracy was around Mars, but he didn't say anything. At least at first.

"What's at the belt?" he finally asked after a long silence.

"Ores going out, supplies going in, and more ships for us."

"I thought Mars was where the action was."

"It was, before Green-Osbourne started their security fleet three years ago. Oh, kid, a word of advice... don't fuck with them. Seriously. Everyone who ever has either died or went to prison when they got out of the hospital."

"Uh, thanks."

They stopped in the Muskie station a few miles away and parked the car. Cheney already had tube tickets.

They rode the Muskie tube half an hour, including a ten minute stop in Springfield, before reaching the spaceport at Scott, outside St. Louis on the Illinois side of the river.

The next day he rode a chemical rocket to low Earth orbit, where he transferred to a fission-powered ion drive ship headed to the asteroid belt. He had no idea what asteroid, and in fact was pretty ignorant about everything about the belt.

The first job he had was cleaning toilets, and they were the filthiest toilets he had ever seen. There weren't enough robots, and in fact the pirates had very few, at least on this ship. He spent the rest of the trip doing similar menial chores that robots usually did.

It took months to get there; the ancient Orion ship the corsairs had stolen was an old fission model that could barely do a quarter gravity, and could only accelerate for a half hour at a time before the engines needed to cool off for twice as long. Newer fusion models could do over half a gravity for an entire trip, and a new GOTS transport could do well over a full gravity, which is why most of the piracy was on Mars—the modern transports could easily outrun pirate boats, so were attacked when they slowed down for a planetary approach.

Finally as he was mopping a floor, an order came over the intercom: “Barnes, Washington, arm yourselves and get to the docking bay. We’re getting a new boat.”

Bobby went to his room, smaller than the prison cell that had previously been home was, and collected the ancient pistol the lead pirate had supplied, grinning widely. The weapon was an antique that used a chemical propellant to fire a projectile. Obsolete, but still deadly as long as its easily manufactured ammunition was available.

This was going to be easy; they’d told him that Orion captains weren’t armed.

And fun. He’d been looking forward to this since prison.

He got to the docking bay, where a third man who Bobby didn’t know was jimmying the lock. “You’re green,” Barnes told Bobby. “I know what I’m doing. I’ll go first.”

The lockpick got the hatch open and Barnes went in, and was hit with a taser. Bobby shot at the captain with the aged weapon and missed. The noise and recoil greatly surprised him; he had never fired it before. Immediately a high pitched whistling sound filled the area—the projectile had pierced the transport’s hull.

His second shot killed the Orion captain, who lay twitching in a widening pool of blood. The taser must not have been very powerful, because Barnes was back on his feet in a couple of minutes, and showed Bobby how to repair a punctured hull. When that was finished, he looked closely at the transport captain’s shirt.

“Damn,” he said. “Not a short shirt. Come on, lets check his quarters.”

"What's a short shirt?"

"It's made of conductive cloth, so tasers won't knock you down. Shorts the tasers out. Been looking for one or two short shirts, maybe some short pants, too. I sure could have used them here!"

"Sounds pretty handy."

"They are. But hey, that's some gun you got there, Washington. Never saw, or heard, anything like it. Man, that thing's loud!"

"Yeah, it surprised me, too. It kind of kicks back when you shoot it, too; made me miss on the first shot."

"Sure leaves a mess!"

"Sure does. I'll trade it for your maser if you want."

Barnes was smarter than Washington and realized it was an antique, probably valuable, and possibly lethal at a far longer range than a maser. They traded weapons, and Bobby was glad to get rid of the heavy, noisy, messy weapon that kicked back so violently when you fired it, and get a quiet, lightweight maser instead.

Masers were great weapons, although they were only good at close range. Any farther than four or five meters away they were pretty much worthless, and were only deadly for a couple of meters, thanks to the Inverse-square law of radio propagation.

The pirates had a new ship. Bobby was determined to get one of his own—or maybe even his own fleet. That was way easier than stealing things on Earth!

Barnes was made captain of the former Orion ship, in charge of a dozen others. Washington stayed on the ship he was on when the raid started.

He was determined to get some short clothes.

"Well, Charles, we have Mars a lot safer than it used to be."

"Yes, Dewey, but Orion lost two transports in the belt this week and Musk lost one last week, too. I think we may need more warships, and better training for our captains. If pirates ever get hold of a GOTS ship, everyone's in trouble."

"Yes, you're right. We need more warships. The fifty we've produced so far aren't enough, but we're turning them out as fast as possible now."

"And more weapons training for cargo and passenger captains. They probably have the most dangerous jobs in the solar system."

Bobby was in the ship's kitchen with three other men, who were talking about a bunch of their rivals ganging up together for the haul of a lifetime—they planned to kidnap Dewey Green's daughter. The rumors were that she, an astrophysicist, was traveling to Mars on a Green-Osbourne ship to build a new kind of telescope.

"Chuckie said they're out of their minds. Says we'll have a lot less competition when those morons are done, and we may find a few stray ships they lose." The pirate chuckled. "I think Chuckie's right. They're crazy, I don't care how many there are, taking on GOTS is suicide."

Jose was on Mars on his first vacation in two years. He'd had the biggest fight of his career six months earlier when more pirates than anyone knew existed tried to apprehend Dewey Green's daughter on a trip from Earth to Mars. It had gotten pretty hairy, especially considering the GOTS transport's cargo. Most of the pirates were killed by the cargo.

Commander Leonard Knapp was in charge of the fleet today, while Jose was on leave, as usual when Captain Ramos wasn't on duty. Both men captained their own ships, and when Ramos was off-duty, Knapp's ship was the flagship. Of course, Ramos' first officer was in charge of Ramos' ship when Ramos was off duty, but Commander Knapp ran the fleet when Ramos was off-duty.

Right then Jose was in the Purple Ruin waiting for the bartender to get to him.

"Can I help you, sir?"

"Yeah, what kind of beer do you have?"

The counterman waved toward the beer taps. "Schotts, Malindar..."

"No, not what brand, what kind? Lager? Pilsner?"

"Hell, I don't know. We have..."

"Give me something in a green bottle."

The barkeep opened the bottle and poured it into a glass, and Jose took a drink. "Hey, that's a great lager! What brand is it?"

"Knolls'."

"Never heard of it."

"Brand new, they just started selling it. Some immigrant from Earth started a Martian brewery. It's way cheaper than the Earthian imports, glad you like it. New on Mars?"

"Yeah, on vacation. I'm with GOTS security."

"Your next beer's on me, then. Damned pirates cost me a ton of money. You guys have things pretty quiet lately. For a while there, as soon as we started loading a shipment from the freighter to the surface, the damned pirates showed up."

"Thanks. We work pretty hard at it."

"Trouble in the belt, I heard, though. Pirates was in here earlier, I heard 'em talkin'."

"You didn't call the authorities?"

"What authorities? Earth doesn't give a damn abut us!"

"Green-Osbourne. And the dome authorities,"

"Huh? Green-Osbourne is just a transportation company, and the dome's cops don't chase pirates unless they're wanted on another dome, or break our laws here. Ain't no laws in space."

"We're authorities on piracy. We've been studying it for a long time. Do you have photos?" he asked, seeing the security cameras.

"Yeah," responded the bartender, who pointed to the cameras that Jose had noticed. "See that dot over the doors, on the ceiling? Those are..."

"Cameras," Jose interrupted. "I saw 'em when I came in."

The tapster's eyes narrowed. "You saw 'em, eh?"

"Sure, part of training. I told you I was with GOTS security, and in fact I'm its head. I was wondering, would the owner mind if you gave me copies of the video of the pirates?"

"Not if you're really with GOTS. Show me some ID and I'll give you the files." Jose did something on his phone, and the bartender did something on his.

"Thanks," Jose said. "We want to build a pirate database; we intend to get rid of piracy completely."

The bartender snickered. "Good luck with *that.*"

Leo was in orbit around Mars, having coffee with William Nigh, the first officer on his ship. "Well, Will, what do you think?"

Nigh sipped his coffee. "I think it's been too quiet. I know there are still pirates."

"Yes, and even if there weren't they could come up at any time. All it takes is a heartless bastard with dreams of riches and a little experience with operating a ship, and they're sure easy to run these days." An alarm went off, and both looked at their phones and hurried to the pilot room.

There was an incoming ship, and it wasn't listed as being on any of the various shipping companies' schedules. Leo looked at his first mate. "Done this before, Will?"

"No."

"Well, you can take it and I'll watch, and give you any pointers after you're done."

"Gotcha." He picked up his phone and closed a contact on the console. "Unknown ship," he said into the phone, "What is your identity, destination, and purpose of travel?"

The radio answered back, through the ship's speakers, "Orion 487 with a load of ferromagnetics for Dome Australia Three."

Nigh quickly keyed "orion 487" into the console, and the screen answered back: it had been missing for two weeks. He spoke into the phone again. "Okay, Captain. We need to make a routine inspection of your ship. Sorry, but it won't take long."

"Roger," the apparent pirate answered, obviously thinking he had fooled Commander Nigh.

Commander Knapp said "Excellent. Well done, Will."

"Fooled that yokel," the ironically named Roger Jolly said, and grabbed his phone. "Everyone get ready for hand to hand, we're taking on GOTS security, but we have the jump on them. They think we're legit. We're gonna get a GOTS!"

Leo aligned his boat with the Orion boat, flanked by half a dozen more GOTS vessels. The pirates had about as much chance as a twentieth century drug gang being raided by a SWAT team. Of course they were fired on by the pirates, and of course Security all wore body armor for protection against projectiles, and electronic armor to neutralize the maser guns most of the privateers were armed with.

Ten men died, twenty were hospitalized, all of them pirates, and the rest went to the orbiting prison the Martian domes' mayors had bankrolled. As usual, the dead pirates were simply jettisoned into space, or "buried at C" as they jokingly called it.

One of the security team was injured by a very loud chemical weapon, but not mortally or permanently. It was a very lucky shot, hitting him in one of the few tiny places a projectile could penetrate.

He would have had a nice scar to show his grandchildren, had he been shot like that a couple hundred years earlier.

Instead, his souvenir was an antique pistol.

Washington felt like he was still in prison. It felt like home. He'd felt like a prisoner as long as he could remember, especially after the first time he'd tried to run away from his initial foster home.

There were five other men on the boat, one they had just stolen from Orion. It was unladen when they got it, but it would be laden soon. Or so its captain hoped.

Its captain was Chuckie—Charles Hunter, recently released from prison, and Bobby had risen to his number two, with his own Orion boat that he didn't really own.

Having his own ship didn't make Bobby feel any less a prisoner.

"Waddle ya have, buddy?" the bartender asked the patron who had just entered.

"Hello, I dunno, maybe a cardinal. Is the manager available?"

"I own the place, will I do?"

"Yes, sir. I'm John Kelly from GOTS security. Just wanted you to know that we're offering cash for information about pirates. We're contacting as many business owners as we can. And besides, I was thirsty."

The bartender snickered. "Everybody's thirsty!" he said, handing the man his Bloody Mary.

Things were starting to become alarmingly routine to Jose, and he didn't like it. Neither did the higher ups who read his reports.

"This isn't good, Dewey," Charles said. "Ramos is right. We have a lot of ships around Mars and not much piracy there, and our competitors are losing a lot of ships in the belt. Their captains aren't trained to fight and their ships aren't equipped to fight.

"And the more pirate ships there are, the more dangerous it is for everyone, us included."

Green looked at a sheet of paper, an object that was supposedly relegated to obsolescence centuries earlier, but somehow was still widely used. "We have two security ships for each of our transports and the transports are fast enough, armed enough, and the captains well trained enough that they're almost impervious to most piracy, anyway."

He thought a few seconds.

"We can profit from this. Sell protection to the other shippers, profit that can make up from the waning profits from returning stolen boats."

Charles snickered. "Those profits aren't down, they're just not up as much as we'd planned. But you're right, that's exactly what we need to do. It will kill several birds with one twenty gauge. I'll get Larry Griffins to get sales on it right away."

"Chuckie" sent Bobby down to Mars for supplies. "Take as much time as you need, Bobby. Here's a phone with enough money on it.

"I'd go with you, but I can't trust any of these other assholes. I'll send Mouse down with you, he's done this before —but make sure he doesn't get hold of that phone!"

Bobby and "Mouse" took a small houseboat down to Mars. It was a four day trip, because they had to evade GOTS.

Mouse was a huge man with bright green eyes and bright red hair, and skin as dark as his hair was bright, two meters tall and weighing a hundred sixty kilograms. His real name was Randall Moore.

"This is a lot easier than it used to be," said Mouse as they approached the red planet. "Only three security vehicles, the rest are in the belt and between here and there. Mars used to be swarming with them."

They landed, showing their counterfeit identification at the spaceport. Counterfeiting documents was far easier than it had been centuries earlier when IDs were all physical, either paper or plastic cards.

"Let me see the phone," Mouse adjured as they walked past the Purple Ruin. "I need to look at the map."

"Sorry, Mouse," Bobby rejoined. "Chuckie gave me strict orders not to. Where are we going, I'll look for it."

"The Purple Onion."

"Isn't that it?" Bobby said, pointing at the bar they had just passed.

Mouse laughed. "No, that's the Purple Ruin, we want the Purple Onion."

"Purple, purple, purple," Bobby muttered. "Are all the damned bars purple?"

"No, just those two. John Purple owns this bar, his brother Harold owns the Onion."

"What's the difference?" Bobby asked while looking for the Purple Onion on his phone. "A bar's a bar."

"Harry's one of us. Emigrated here ten years ago, had gone to school with Chuckie. We'd probably get killed in the Ruin, it's affiliated with one of our competitors, and in fact," he said chuckling, "We've even taken some of their boats and loads. They hate our guts."

The statement that they would be killed in the Purple Ruin was nonsense; there had never been a known murder on Mars in its entire history; space was where the carnage was, not on Mars or any other body except Earth. On Earth, it was mainly pirates and other gangsters and the angel tear addicts who were violent. In space, it was just the pirates, as dropheads hated low gravity, let alone microgravity.

They got to the address the phone sent them to, but rather than the Purple Onion, the sign outside read "Captain Hooker's". The purple trim on the doors and windows had been painted white.

"Well, I'll be damned," Mouse said. "This is where it was. Maybe Harry just changed the name."

They went in, and Mouse asked the Japanese bartender if Harry was there.

"No," she replied with a thick accent, "He get arrested three week ago and is waiting in jail for his case to come to trial. The city confiscated the bar and sold it to a new immigrant. You want drink?"

"Yeah," Mouse said, "shot of whiskey and a beer."

"What kind?"

"The good stuff. How 'bout you, Bobby?"

"Just a beer, I guess. Guinness."

She looked doleful. "Sorry, sir, we no have right now. Supplies short until next month when new shipment come."

"I don't care, then," Washington replied. "Anything. Whatever you have on draft."

As she was pouring their beer and Mouse's shot, Bobby said "Shit. What now?"

Mouse shook his head. "Dunno. We'll just pick up what we can in this dome and go back, I guess."

They each drank another beer and left. The woman picked up her phone. "GOTS," she said.

"GOTS," the phone replied. "How can I help you?"

"Two men in Hooker's a minute ago I think be pirates, ask for previous owner. Here their pictures," she said, doing something with the phone. "You should now have their identities, not just photos."

Jose, with a week left on his vacation, was back in the Purple Ruin sipping his first beer when his phone went off. He was informed that the local law enforcement had been called about some pirates, both of whom were wanted on Earth for parole violations. He left his half beer on the bar with a tip equal to the beer's cost and hurried outside, asking his phone "Location of Robert Luther Washington."

The phone informed him where Bobby was. Jose thought that name seemed familiar, but couldn't place where he'd heard it. Ah, just a common first and last name, he thought.

He reached the store the computer told him he'd find the pirates, but instead of pirates he found two police officers handcuffed to a rail with their own handcuffs, and gagged with cloth tape, and a sales clerk tied and gagged with the same tape; tape that was sold in the store.

"That will be two seventy seven," the clerk told the two pirates when they laid the goods on the counter.

"Even?"

"Yes sir," the clerk answered.

Bobby pulled out the phone as a voice behind him sternly said "Hands up and don't move."

Bobby whirled around as the taser darts hit him, to no avail—he and Mouse were wearing short shirts.

Mouse lifted one of the policemen with one hand, Bobby kneed the other in the groin, and struck him hard in the face three times as the clerk reached for his phone. The huge man grabbed the clerk as Bobby handcuffed the policeman he had incapacitated, and then the other cop Mouse was holding.

They tied up the clerk with tape, taped up all three of their mouths, hurriedly bagged up what they had paid for and quite a bit more they hadn't, and hightailed it out of there before slowing down, so as to not attract attention, fearful that they already had.

Outside the store, Mouse handed Bobby a sheet of foil. "Here," he said, "wrap the phone up in this."

"Why?"

"So they can't track us."

He wrapped up the phone as they walked swiftly to the houseboat, and took off as soon as they could ready the craft.

"Man," Mouse said, "that was close. Chuckie was right, you're a damned good fighter. I wouldn't want to have to take you on."

Bobby snorted.

Jose removed the tape from the three men's mouths while calling the local police with their communications devices, and asked them as he was untaping the clerk, "where are your handcuff keys?"

"Pirates took 'em, along with our phones and tasers," one of the officers said with a raspy voice. His throat was bruised.

The other lawman, who if he was bruised it didn't show because of his very dark complexion, said "Somebody ought to be here pretty quick with keys. Man, my balls hurt. I think that guy was on drops!"

"The one that got me sure didn't need drops, he was bigger'n a elephant. I doubt the other one was on them, droppers are only dangerous when they're withdrawing."

"Then why didn't my taser do anything? It must have been drops!"

"Why didn't mine?"

"I don't know."

"Short clothes," Jose said.

"Huh?" Both cops said in unison.

"Short shirts and short pants. All of our passenger vessel captains wear them in case a traveler goes nuts and gets hold of his taser. Pirates surely have them now, they've killed so many boat captains and stolen so many ships. You fellows dealt with those two before?"

"No. You, Bill?"

"No, but the computer says they're both wanted on Earth; USA, Illinois. Jumped parole, disappeared as soon as they got out of prison. They've been looking for them for a really long time now."

Jose replied "They should have stayed on Earth. Pirates die young."

"What kind of trouble?" Chuckie asked.

"All kinds. First off, Harry got busted."

"What?"

"Yeah, his bar had a different name and a Jap chick who was tending bar said he'd been busted and was in jail, and that the dome had confiscated his bar and sold it to some new immigrant. Don't know how they found out about him, maybe his brother snitched.

"Then *we* almost got busted buying supplies in a store. Martian police with tasers, we bested 'em and got the hell off the planet. We got most of what we needed except food."

Chuckie grinned. "Good, saved me a ton of money. We just copped an O'Riley's freighter full of beef and frozen vegetables on its way from Earth to Ceres. Considering the trouble you had, you boys did damned good! You guys ever ate pork before?"

Jose couldn't get Robert Washington's name off his mind, and the picture seemed familiar, too, but Jose couldn't figure it out. It ate at him, illogically, he knew, but it still did.

Oh, well. Leave was up in a week and he could stop thinking about this meaningless stuff and think about stuff that mattered.

But who the hell was this Robert Washington and why did he seem so damned familiar?

"Okay, Me, Bobby and Jack hold back while John and Winkie attack."

"Why?"

Chuckie's eyes narrowed. "Who the hell are you? You work for me?"

"Yeah, I'm running John's boat 'cause he has the bottle flu. You want it back, it's yours."

"So what's your problem?"

"Why you holding back?" His eyes narrowed, obviously distrustful and cautious.

"Two waves. We want to win. Got a problem with that?

"I guess not. But what's your plan?"

"Some of those supplies Bobby and Mouse got were for making an EMP. Your boat shoots at him with rockets and lasers and Winkie will get close to him and set off the EMP. Then you dock with Winkie, let him in your boat, and ready Winkie's boat for towing to our yards when we're done. I'll tow the Musk boat."

The man grinned. "Chuckie, you're a God damned genius!"

"Yeah? Maybe not if it's a decoy and there ain't no ore. I got a buyer for that ore. The ship is junk, Musk ships ain't worth shit."

Jose briefed his troops about their upcoming mission, protecting a Musk Enterprises transport carrying Cererian ore to Mars. Musk was paying quite a bit for GOTS protection, as the previous three attempted shipments had all been hijacked and their insurance company had dropped their theft coverage. The GOTS contract put all liability on Green-Osbourne.

They would follow a thousand kilometers behind the Musk vessel. Green-Osbourne ships were almost invisible, and in fact were invisible to all but another GOTS boat; GOTS captains knew there were ions being released in the exhaust.

The Musk ship was slow, and ten days into the trip Jose saw the "bogeys" coming in. He lessened the distance between his and the Musk transport.

Security vehicles carried no atomics; they didn't want to destroy vessels unless necessary. But GOTS transports carried them.

And in this case, as with others, they couldn't use an EMP close to the Musk vessel unless it was in danger of being destroyed.

The pirate fleet wasn't close enough for its lasers to do any harm to the Musk transport, but they were firing them anyway. Lasers aren't like high speed projectiles. In space, projectiles keep their kinetic energy until hitting a target, while a laser is victim of the inverse square law and loses energy with distance.

Ramos fired rail slugs at the ship that was firing on the Musk vessel. It's hard to hit anything at the distances between space ships with a rail gun, although if it has enough power to do damage a laser seldom misses, but it was too far for a laser blast to do any damage.

The slug missed, and Jose fired again.

A different vessel was coming from a different direction, and Jose targeted it with lasers and put them under computer control.

There was a flash outside the Musk ship, and the lights went out on the Musk ship and the two pirate craft.

"Bobby! Holy shit, It's GOTS security! Get us the hell out of here!"

"You don't have to tell me twice," he replied, as he was indeed already "getting the hell" out of there, as were the other two boats.

"Damn," Chuckie swore. "Dam damn DAMN IT! Those were two shitty boats but a boat's a boat!!"

"What about their crews?"

"So what about them? That's the breaks, son. Head for Vesta, we need supplies and I don't think GOTS is guarding it right now; no shipments scheduled for three weeks."

"How do you know?"

Chuckie smiled. "We got our spies. We got spies in every dome!"

Jose rescued the Musk captain and his crew made Musk's crippled craft ready for towing, and waited, drifting at a high rate of speed, for three tow tugs to show up and take the vessels to Mars for repairs, and for the two stolen craft to be returned to the companies who owned them—for a hefty fee, of course.

His ship accompanied the tugs to Mars. They supplied life support equipment in the two stolen transports after the pirates would have been unconscious. They would eventually wind up in the orbiting Martian prison, or in prison on Earth if they were wanted there.

"Godamnit!! Billy, Jack, grab that son of a bitch!"

Chuckie was frantic. One of his less distrusted captains was trying to steal one of his stolen boats.

"Kill his boat?"

"Hell, no! Latch on, get in, and kill the dickweed!"

The pirate who tried to steal the pirate's stolen boat died.

The ship's electronics died as well, which was unfortunate, but could be repaired.

Unlike the dead pirate, which was only unfortunate for the dead pirate.

"So, Mouse, been on Vesta before? We affiliated with this bar?

"No, we got no bars on Vesta, but the drinks are cheap and a lot of the boys we deal with come here. Just don't let the barkeep get wise."

George Armstrong was captain of a Musk transport carrying Vestan nickle and iron ores to Mars' smelting plants. Jose's GOTS security ship would escort Armstrong's craft to Mars, protecting it from pirates. Jose was on Vesta, in the Rotgut Saloon.

Yes, that was its name, a sort of Vestan joke. Vestans had an unearned reputation of being drunken brawlers, probably because the original settlers in its dome were Irish immigrants from Earth. The other two bars had similar offensively humorous names.

He'd been in this bar before, as GOTS was covering asteroids and Vesta and Ceres now, as well as Mars. Jose, now a captain, was leader of the six hundred craft security fleet. It was over three times as large as Green-Osbourne's shipping and traveling fleet, as GOTS revenues from protecting other shippers was now larger than profits from their own shipping vessels.

"Waddle it be, mighty?" the obviously Australian... British? ...bartender asked.

"You have Knolls' Lager?"

"Sure, on tap."

"Okay, a pint of Knolls Lager."

Just then George walked in. "You again!" he exclaimed, grinning.

"Hi, George," Jose replied, standing up and extending his hand, which George shook. "Yep, me again. We leave orbit at noon tomorrow?"

"Yeah, and I have to tell you, I'm sure glad it's your boat that's guarding us!"

Jose poo-poohed the idea. "Nah, any of our boats would have been fine."

"Yeah," George said with a grin, "But..."

"Son of a bitch!" Jose interrupted. "Randall Moore. God damned pirate" he exclaimed, pulling his taser from his pocket. "You! You're under arrest!"

Mouse tried to reach in a pocket; Bobby was in the rest room, having drank half a six pack. Jose hit Mouse with a taser, to no effect. Mouse pulled his maser, to no more effect except that the Musk transport captain and the bartender screamed. Luckily for them, they were close enough for pain but not long term damage. Jose had his electronic shield turned on.

The very large man pulled a very large knife that looked strangely small in his huge hand, with the blade swinging out before he lunged.

Mouse was big, but Jose was well trained and it took little time to subdue him. During the ruckus, Bobby slipped out the back door, remembering Chickie's admonition: "Don't fuck with GOTS security." Anybody who could take a guy like Mouse *must* be GOTS security.

The dome police came in and took Moore into custody. Jose sat back down next to George. "You okay, buddy? My shield should have covered everybody!"

The bartender said "Masers are highly directional, like a laser, only microwave frequencies instead of optical frequencies. The guy was just a piss-poor shot."

"Speaking of shots," Jose said, still panting, "give me a shot of rum, I don't care what brand."

The planets' and asteroids' orbits at the time were such that Hebe was on the way to Mars. Hebe's dome wasn't even finished yet, and as well as rare earths for Mars, George and Jose were to drop a load of food on Hebe for the workers there. They encountered no pirates on the voyage.

Hebe's extremely low gravity made it possible for George to land the giant transport for offloading; even Ceres was light enough. Jose and his crew orbited the asteroid, on the lookout for buccaneers. Leo was captain of his own ship elsewhere, and Lieutenant Commander Ken Johnson, a dark skinned man with short, tightly curled hair was Jose's second in command.

"Ever been on the surface of Hebe, Ken?"

"No, why?"

"I know how it got its name."

"How?"

"It has less than one percent of Earth's gravity, but there's still a small pull. Gives you the heebie-jeebies."

Jose was completely wrong about this. Hebe was named two hundred years before people ever visited space, let alone before visiting the asteroids, which like other bodies orbiting the sun was named from ancient Greek and Roman mythology. In this case it was the "bartender to the gods".

However, in the early twenty first century they seemed to have found that Hebe had a satellite, which they jokingly named "Jebe".

Johnson started chuckling, and stopped suddenly. "Uh, oh. We have an 'unannounced,' Jose." Ken closed a contact on the panel and spoke into his phone. "Craft en-route to Hebe, who are you and what is your business here?"

The answer came a couple of minutes later; there's a bit of radio lag with the distances. "Picking up supplies. Who are you and why do you care?"

Ken looked at Jose, who said "get rid of him. With George down there on Hebe he's vulnerable, and we can't go chasing pirates."

Johnson spoke to the obvious picaroons. "We're Green-Osbourne Transportation Systems Security and there are no supplies for you at Hebe. Leave now or die!"

Jose laughed. "Think it'll work?"

"If they don't think I'm lying. We're too close to the asteroid for an EMP." It would disable George and the equipment used for building the new dome.

Chuckie swore a string of incredibly loud and foul obscenities, followed by "what a shitty, shitty week. We lost fifteen ships and their crews, we lost Mouse, and damn but that big guy was valuable to us.

"Damn! I wouldn't think GOTS would be guarding a facility with no boats and no production yet, and we need tools and food. We're going to have to risk Mars."

"We are?"

"Sure thing, Bobby, you and me."

"Who's going to guard the ship?"

"I'll land on Phobos. Nobody will find it there."

"How do we know that was really GOTS?"

"We don't, but we don't know they're not and we can't afford to take any chances. I've sent my captains after new boats. We need to recruit, somehow. I'll think of something."

"How are you going to keep those assholes from stealing their boats while we're on Mars?"

Chuckie grinned. "I had a guy rattle around in the engine rooms. Told the captains that the ships were rigged to blow up in three weeks if they're not stopped by a gizmo I have."

"Are they?"

"I wish they were, but the threat is enough."

George was waiting in Captain Hooker's for his old friend from the rival company. Jose was in his houseboat on his way down; his ship was at the dockyards in orbit for routine maintenance.

"You not from Mars, are you?" the bartender said as she handed George his beer.

"No, I'm from Kansas City. How can you tell?

"Martians seem to be, I don't know, not skinnier but less muscle. Vacation?"

"No, I captain a Musk transport ship. My buddy Jose's meeting me here, he's on his way now. My company hired his company to protect my shipment, and I'm sure glad they did.

"Hey, didn't I see you last year at the Purple Ruin?"

She grinned. "Yeah, he not good. John pay better."

Bobby and Chuckie came in as George sipped his beer, checking the time on his phone. Not knowing that the bartender had pegged them as pirates earlier, and in fact didn't recognize her, they ordered beers. Chuckie asked the bartender where she was from.

"Tsushima."

"Huh? Where's that?"

"It a small city in Japan. Hate crowds in Japan so I be here now. No crowds on Mars."

"Small city and crowded?"

"Tiny, not much more than a million people. No have farms any more, all industry. Farms all be inside buildings now in Japan."

Just then Jose finally walked in. “There you are, you old rascal, you!” George exclaimed.

“Hey, George, you old rapscallion you!”

Down the bar, Bobby recognized Jose. “Oh, shit,” he swore softly, “That guy that just came in is the guy that got Mouse!”

“Oh, hell,” Chuckie said, pulling out he maser.

“He’s got a shield. We need to get the hell out of here!”

They got up silently and tried to sneak past the captains. They were unsuccessful.

“Shit!” Jose exclaimed, and pulled out two tasers. The pirates started to run, but Jose hit them both in the back of the head with taser darts.

They should have been wearing short hats.

“So you’re a free man tomorrow, Rick. What are your plans?”

“Hell, Bobby, I don’t know. Robin’ folks, I guess. I sure ain’t gonna settle for bein’ poor. No jobs after a place like this. I’ll probably be back in two weeks.”

“No you won’t,” Bobby replied. “I got a job for you. See Ron Cheney, he’ll pick you up at the gate when they let you out. I’ve seen you fight, we could use you.”

"I imagine you're all pretty disappointed, professor?"

"Well, of course, Mister Wussman. We were sure this system would have life present, even intelligent life."

"Why was that, Doctor Fielgud? Did you detect electromagnetic communications or something?"

"Of course not. Any electromagnetic communications would be completely drowned out by the radiation from the system's star. 'Listening' for electromagnetic radiation is futile; no way would we ever hear another intelligence's electromagnetic communication, and even if we did it would appear to be random noise."

"Why would it appear to be random noise?"

"How would we decode it? We can't even decode our own prehistoric writings from the arthrolothic age without some sort of clue. Were it not for the bugatti stone, we never would have been able to interpret the Argostnic's writings."

The reporter shifted in her chair a little, if it could indeed be called a chair. "But doctor, why is it that astronomers had such high hopes for finding life in this stellar system?"

"Well, Mister Wussman, you must realize that finding any kind of extraforgostnic life, even bacteria, would be forgost shattering? We haven't found life anywhere but here on forgost. Not even single cells, not even the most primitive. But this was so promising."

"Again, professor, why was this system so special?"

Professor Wussman's uthropids wiggled in annoyance, and he was immediately embarrassed by his uncharacteristic show of emotion. The doctor was proud of his aloofness. "It has four planets, three of them in the 'Goldilocks' zone, and all of them have many sizeable satellites, most suitable for life as we know it. There is water and methane on many of them."

"What about planetoids? Moon-sized objects without planets to orbit?"

"Life can't form on a planetoid. You need tidal forces to stir the chemicals, or life simply can't form."

"I read your paper, sir, as much of it as I could understand, but isn't one of the planetoids a double planetoid? Wouldn't the tidal forces be great enough there?"

"Yes, the third orbit around the star has a double planetoid, and theoretically the tidal forces would be great enough for life to form. Unfortunately, they're far too close to the star to support life; the gamma radiation is far too great. It would be like the entire planetoid being made of uranium and trapped in a gaint X-Ray machine. Plus, its atmosphere is very high in oxygen, most likely from stellar radiation breaking the water into hydrogen and oxygen. And oxygen is a deadly poison. Nothing could live there."

"So this system is tapped out?"

"Yes, we've examined every single satellite of the three planets and come up empty. But we're looking at other stellar systems with bodies large enough to be called 'planets' with inhabitable satellites, and we're sure to find life."

"So you're convinced that forgost isn't the only planetary satellite that has life?"

"I'm certain of it. As large as the galaxy is, it's a mathematical certainty that we'll find life somewhere. We just have to keep looking."

"What do you think intelligent extraforgostnic life would be like, Doctor Fielgud?"

"It's not likely they would be anything like us. Forget the science fiction shows that have many alien species having sex with each other and even reproducing, with all of them having four walking appendages, four grasping appendages, and four electromagnetic sensors."

"The show *Wiersman's Planet* has an intelligent bipedal species; original, but it doesn't seem very realistic. Do you think any extraforgostnic aliens could be bipedal?"

"Not flarging likely! For all we know, intelligent alien life could be bipedal, but that would be incredibly unlikely—walking on only two appendages and still being able to think of anything but falling down would be pretty unbelievable."

"Well, thank you for the interview, Doctor Fielgud, it was good of you to come today."

"Thank you, Mister Wussman."

Wussman turned to the electromagnetic recognizer. "And now a word from our sponsor..."

"Wild Bill! Damn, what a surprise! Why didn't you call?"

"Because then it wouldn't have been a surprise! Give me a Newcastle, I haven't had a beer in nine months! How've you been, you old pirate killer?"

"I'm doing great, just graduated business school two months ago. The bar is doing real good, and Destiny and her team have almost finished building that new kind of telescope. You sure you want Newcastle?"

"Huh? Your Newcastle went bad?"

"Here, you old asshole, have one of mine on the house," John said, pouring from a tapper to a beer mug. "Tell me what you think. There's nothing wrong with my Newcastle stock but I'll bet you won't want Newcastle after you try this."

Bill eyed the mug warily. "Import?" He took a sip. "Pretty good!" He took another sip. "You were right! This is some damned good beer. What country was it imported from?"

"Mars, you asshole. I built a microbrewery here. At least, it started as a microbrewery, it's a lot bigger now. Hell, I'm thinking of exporting it to Earth."

"What? Bullshit, you're full of shit, you old bullshitter. Come on, you can't bullshit a bullshitter. After shipping it would cost ten times what Newcastle cost!"

"Yep, just like Newcastle is ten times what Knolls' cost here."

"Forgswaggle!"

"Young man!" an old woman at the other end of the bar admonished, "Watch your fucking language, asshole!"

Bill turned red as a beet. "Oh shit, I'm sorry, Ma'am, I didn't see you down there, I thought just John and me was here."

"Well, just watch it, dickhead."

"Yes ma'am." He turned back to John.

"But who in the hell would be buying it?"

"Who do you think? People who eat pork. I hear they're smuggling my beer all over the damned solar system, but mostly to Earth. It will probably take a few years before I can expand enough for exports, though. I can barely keep up with Martian demand."

"Damn, you must be doing good. What's with that giant framed picture of a guy in an eighteenth century pirate costume with a parrot on his shoulder and playing a guitar?"

"It's a photo of an old blues guy centuries ago, John Lee Hooker, with the pirate stuff added in a computer."

"Your last run. The one with all them damned pirates. Now I get it. Damn, that was pretty scary. I didn't think I'd make it back to Mars. At least, until the fleet reached me. You were pretty far ahead..."

"Well, DUH, you were on batteries."

"Yeah, the pirates showed up right when the fleet did. I thought I'd get boarded. Scared the fognart out of me!"

"YOUNG MAN!!!"

"Oops, shit, I forgot. I'm sorry, ma'am."

"Spew shit out of your mouth again, young man, and I'm kicking your God damned ass."

"Sorry, ma'am."

"Fuck you."

He turned back to John, his red face a little less red. “Hey, sell me a half dozen kegs. I have to go back to Saturn and that’s a long damned way.”

“Sorry, Bill, I ain’t gonna do it.”

“What?? What the fuck, John?”

“Sorry, Bill, but I lost too many friends already, damn them fucking pirates. I almost lost Gus thanks to my stupidity and I’ll be damned if I’m going to be responsible for your dying. I ain’t got enough friends to lose any more, especially you.”

“John, what in the blagsphorth are...”

“YOUNG MAN!!!”

“Oops, fuck, I’m sorry, ma’am. I keep forgetting.”

“Just watch your fucking mouth, boy.”

“Yes, ma’am. John, what the FUCK are you talking about?”

“I’m talking about Gus. I almost killed him!”

“Gus? Blagforth...”

“YOUNG MAN! I’m not listening to this garbage!” The old woman stomped out.

“Blagforth forgnart, Bill, that’s one of my best patrons, spends a fortune getting blagforthfaced in here.”

“Gee, John, I don’t want to cause you any lost business...”

“Garp that old crant,” John said. “It’s a fognarth fucking bar. If she don’t want to hear vulgar language she can drink somewhere else.”

“Why won’t you sell me that beer?”

“I told you, because of Gus. I almost killed him.”

“What the fognarth are you talking about?”

“Gus came through about six months ago or so. I hadn’t seen him in a long damned time, he hadn’t had any Martian runs. Anyway, he wanted beer, Loved my Captain Hooker’s Pale Ale...”

“What am I drinking?”

“Lager. Anyway, he wanted fifteen barrels. I didn’t think nothing of it, but he was drunk on his approach to Mars and the God damned pirates, as few as there are left, almost got him. I almost killed Gus and I’ll be damned if I’m going to kill you!”

“Fognarth blagsphorth, John, you fucking asshole. Yeah, you shouldn’t have sold beer to Gus. Shit, that asshole is an alcoholic. What the fucking blagsphorth is wrong with you, asshole? Jesus, John. You’re a fucking moron.”

“Well, garp, I guess you’re not Gus. Okay, I’ll sell you the garping beer, motherfucker. But God damned fognarth, you better not garping die!”

It was a beautiful spring day on the riverfront. Pleasant temperatures, white puffy clouds floating in a bright blue sky, and the bright sunshine gleaming off of the enormous arch made it seem the perfect day and spot for a picnic. There were a lot of people there, enjoying the weather, walking, having picnics.

Everything changed in an instant. An automobile leaped off the ground and came crashing down on another car, narrowly missing the Smiths, who were on their way from Indianapolis to enjoy their honeymoon in Vegas.

Another car went flying, and of course everyone was running and screaming in panic—but the cause of all the bent metal and broken glass was a mystery.

Bob Capone, a sergeant in the St. Louis police force, was there on duty, talking with his friend John Jennings of the National Parks Service. Both whipped out their radios, calling for help.

Another car leaped into the air and crashed down on a different one, and both burned when the sparks from the collision ignited the gasoline that had spilled out of several.

The cars then stopped pretending to be frogs. Five minutes later a car driving north on interstate 44 stopped suddenly in front of the Old Cathedral Museum and bounced back, the front of the auto smashed, as if it had struck an invisible and immobile object.

The destruction continued down Market Street for an hour, and stopped abruptly at Seventh as National Guard helicopters swooped in.

The aircraft hovered for an hour or two, but there was no further damage.

The local news media had a field day. This was Big, big with a capital B. The national and world news would be covering this, and the local news men and women all thought "This is it! My career is going to skyrocket!"

The next day, General Ferguson (whose name was uncomfortably the same as a town in the greater metropolitan area) was in an incredibly bad mood, so of course all of his underlings were, as well.

"Well, Colonel? What happened? Who has it and how did he get it?"

"Well, sir, the investigation is underway. We're not sure what happened but... well, sir, we believe a unit was stolen. We don't know who stole it, but it was probably an inside job."

"Terrorists?"

"Unknown, sir, but improbable. It appears that there was no loss of life and few injuries, the worst being broken bones. It's mostly property damage."

"Do we know who has it and where it is?"

"No, sir, not yet. Should I alert the civilian authorities to what they're up against?"

"Under no circumstances will that happen unless the President himself orders it. This is top secret and will remain that way."

"Yes, sir."

"What are we doing about the situation?"

"We're loading firefighting helicopters with paint. When it strikes again we'll have an idea where it is, and when it's painted we'll be able to see it. We have men manning the two other units, they should be able to stop it."

"Very well, Colonel. Make sure no one without a top secret clearance sees it when it's painted. Dismissed." The Colonel saluted and left.

The next day, Sergeant Capone was back down by the waterfront. The entire metropolitan area was on alert, and the President had declared martial law in Missouri and Illinois. People were ordered to stay in their homes, as if their homes would protect them from something that could throw cars.

His radio came on—he was being ordered back to the station. Curious. As he walked towards his squad car it suddenly left the ground and was hurling straight at him, barely missing.

Helicopters swooped down, and the invisible monster disappeared. Sergeant Capone radioed that his squad car had been totaled, and was informed that another car would come to pick him up. A couple of hours later the helicopters departed.

"Well, Colonel?"

"We're pretty sure we know who it is, sir. Corporal George Smith is AWOL, called in sick yesterday and didn't show up for work this morning. We checked his quarters, he wasn't home and his car was on-base.

"And we think we know what made him snap—his brother was an undercover narcotics officer and was accidentally killed in a gun battle with an off-duty St. Louis police officer. Neither knew the other was a law enforcement officer.

"We think he's out for revenge, sir. Twice he's struck the same area, an area where the other law enforcement officer has his beat. So we have helicopters standing by at LaClede's Landing, camouflaged, of course.

"Unfortunately, we had a fatality yesterday. A police officer got in a gun battle with troops clearing the street and was killed."

"Unfortunate, indeed. How long until Smith runs out of food or water, or the unit runs out of power?"

"Power will last about a week, food and water longer."

"I want you to get with engineering, when we get it back we need to find a way to keep this from happening again. Is that all, Colonel?"

"Yes, sir."

"Okay, you're dismissed."

Things were quiet the next two days, and social media started to grumble.

The General got a missive from the President himself, he was to meet with one of the President's people.

General Ferguson called the St. Louis Chief of Police. "We need your help. We know what it is, but we can't tell you. I'd like to have Sergeant Capone on the waterfront today."

"I'm sorry, General, but I don't think you have the authority to give me that order. You're going to have to speak to the mayor."

"Sgt. Capone, can I see you in my office?"

"Of course."

"Close the door, would you?"

"What's this about, Lieutenant?"

"Damn it, Bob, don't give me that 'Lieutenant' crap, we've been friends since high school. What the hell is going on?"

Capone was puzzled. "Joe, I have no idea what you're talking about. What the hell *are* you talking about?"

"Damn it, Bob, what the hell did you do? Why does the mayor want to talk to you?"

"What? Why would he want to talk to *me*? Come on, Joe, tell me what this is all about."

"His assistant wouldn't say. Anyway, you need to get down there right now, the guy from the mayor's office sounded scared. Let me know what's going on. I hope you're not in trouble."

"Me, too, but I don't know what I would be in trouble for. I'll let you know."

"Okay, get your ass down there!"

"Can I help you, Sergeant?

"I was told the mayor wanted to see me. I..."

"Sgt. Capone?"

"Yes, ma'am."

"Oh, please follow me, he's waiting for you."

The mayor was with an Army general in uniform. He stood quietly as the mayor spoke. "Sergeant, the president called me."

Bob was puzzled but silent. The mayor continued hesitantly. "Sergeant, all I know is it's vital for national security that you do whatever General Ferguson asks. Will you do that, Sergeant?"

Of course he said "yes". Only an idiot would answer otherwise. The general looked at the mayor. The mayor said "Excuse me" and left.

"You were in the service?" the general asked.

"Yes, sir. Air Force."

"Why didn't you re-up?"

"I didn't want to be a bubble chaser, I wanted to be a cop."

"A bubble chaser? What's that?"

"A hydraulics technician. We were 'bubble chasers', electricians were 'spark chasers', the..."

"Did you have any kind of clearance?"

"Clearance?"

"Security clearance."

"Oh, yes, sir. I worked on some of the stealth aircraft. I thought you fellows would have looked that up."

"What kind of aircraft?"

"I'm sorry, sir, I can't discuss them."

The general grinned broadly. "Excellent. Yes, we did look it up. All of this is on a 'need to know' basis. We're dealing with some top secret gear.

"I can't tell you what's going on, of course, but you need to know we need you as bait."

"Bait? For what, sir?"

"I can't tell you. All you need to know is that we're going down to the riverfront and you need to stick as close to me as possible."

A knock came from the door and the general answered it, and was given a sheet of printed paper. He glanced at it, and said "Please wait here, Sergeant. I'll be back shortly."

He walked down the hall, where an aide told him "The units are ready, sir."

"Thank you, Lieutenant." He changed into a police officer's uniform and collected Sgt. Capone. They drove to the riverfront in a police cruiser, got out, walked a few yards and stopped.

Capone noticed the general's strange weaponry, but knew better than to ask about it. It looked to him like a paintball gun. Laser? Maybe. This whole experience was very strange, he thought.

The day was uneventfully boring.

It was far from boring at the police station; all hell was breaking loose. Several squad cars were destroyed, and the police were close to panic. It lasted for maybe twenty minutes, and the destruction stopped when the helicopters showed up.

The mayor appeared on the television news that night, assuring residents that the next day the police would all be on their normal assigned duties but the curfew was still in place until the president ordered otherwise.

The next morning General Ferguson and Sgt. Capone were back down by the riverfront. An hour later a car became animated, hurling itself through the air at the general and the policeman. Capone ran and the general kept firing his paint gun.

His fourth shot splattered in the air, becoming an animated blob the general could see flying through the air. He kept firing until his gun was out of paint.

There was an awful racket coming from the flying blobs, the sound of heavy steel on heavy steel.

"Capone!" the general ordered. "Back to the station, I'll take it from here."

The Sergeant mulled over what he had seen as he was driving back to the station. It looked to him after it was splattered with paint like it was some kind of giant headless humanoid robot. He wondered what it was, but knew he would never know for sure, but the military seemed to have found a way to make objects invisible in visible light.

He went to see the lieutenant as soon as he got back. The lieutenant had him close the door. "So what's going on, Bob?"

"Sorry, Joe, it's a military secret and I'm not allowed to talk about it."

"Well, at least I know you're not in trouble. The mayor called, you're getting some kind of medal or award or something, so I guess I should say 'good work'."

Down by the riverfront an Army tech sergeant was unlocking the paint spattered, otherwise invisible machine, pistol drawn and at the ready. After looking inside he holstered his pistol and called down to the general. "He's dead, sir. Apparently shot himself, there's a hell of a bloody mess inside the unit."

The general ordered that the two invisible units put all three units in a semitrailer to be shipped back to the base.

That evening the president was on the television news, praising the Army and police Sergeant Bob Capone, and informing everyone that the danger was passed and the curfew was lifted. The mayor came on and praised the city police force in general and Bob Capone in particular.

"Re-enlist..." Bob thought. "Nonsense, I'd far rather chase criminals than bubbles. I hate working on hydraulics!"

Mayor Waldo was eating his salad as he waited for the main course when he was summoned to Dome Hall for an emergency. His secretary insisted that he couldn't talk about it in public or on the phone.

He paid for the meal, told the serverbot to keep his food warm when it was finished cooking, and returned to Dome Hall, muttering under his breath. He asked Willie Clark, his secretary, what was going on that was so important it would interrupt his lunch hour.

"A body was found outside the dome, sir. We suspect murder."

Murder? There had been a lot of death in Mars' hundred years of colonization, but until now there hadn't been a single murder, at least that anyone had known about. There were no homicides on the planet's surface, at least; in space the pirates would kill you the first chance they got. In space, only the Green-Osbourne Transportation Company's security fleet kept things relatively calm.

"Why do you suspect murder? There's never been a murder on Mars."

"Until now. The body was found outside the dome and wasn't wearing a suit."

"Maybe he was drunk and stumbled through the wrong door. I should talk to council members about assigning guards to the airlocks."

"No, sir. Impossible. The body was found a half kilometer from the nearest lock. If he'd simply walked through the airlock..."

"Hmm, yes. He'd have died before he went two steps and probably would have died inside the lock. Who do you have investigating?"

"Nobody yet, sir. The police chief called us right before we called you, looking for guidance. The coroner is examining the body and we expect her report in a week or two. The corpse had been out there a couple of days at least. Of course there was no decay, but the body was completely desiccated, freeze-dried, as would be expected."

"Do we know the cause of death? Was a dead body taken outside, or a live one out there to die?"

"The coroner is still doing the examination, sir. We'll let you know as soon as we know."

"Thanks, Willie. Have the police start an investigation, and have them get in touch with an Earthian police detective who has experience in solving homicides, and have our people get advice from him or her."

"Should we keep this secret? At least until we know more? The Chief thinks so."

"No, you're not working for Wilcox any more, and I'm not anything like Wilcox was. That's why we won in a landslide, people hated his secrecy. Set up a press conference for tomorrow morning."

"Yes, sir."

He went back and finished his lunch.

Albert Morton was the electrician who had discovered the body. It had been the most horrible thing he had ever seen in his life, and it ate at him that there had been nothing about it on the news. Who had done this, and why? He decided to contact a newspaper the next morning. Tonight he was going to get drunk; he'd never seen anything so gruesome, and couldn't get the awful scene out of his head.

"Say, Ed, how's being Mayor treating you? Lager?"

"Hi, John. Yeah, and a shot, I don't care what. Scotch, I guess. My job's sure not very fun today, we're almost certain that we have a murder on our hands."

"Murder? On Mars? Really?"

"We can't see how it could be anything else. He was found half a kilometer from the airlock without an environment suit."

"What killed him?"

"We won't know until the coroner's report comes in. But it has to be murder, nothing else makes sense. How's business?"

"I just got mail from Dewey this morning. We captured five pirate vessels last week and got a nice big finder's fee from the boats' rightful owners. He and Charles are looking at some new propulsion systems that might be a lot more efficient than the ion engines we're using now. That will both lower the shipper's cost and increase our profits, maybe even more than when we went from fission generators to fusions. And there's a lot more shipping since they found all those rare earths on Ceres."

"Your bar doesn't seem to be doing all that good."

John snorted. "You know this is just a hobby, but still, it is turning a small profit. It doesn't usually get too busy until later at night. My brewery is doing almost too good. It's hard to grow enough ingredients to brew enough of it to supply the demand. I may have to buy another building to grow more hops and barley and so forth. I still have to import some, even with the farm."

A man walked in. "Hi, Al," the bartender said. "The usual?"

"Not today, John. Really bad day, I'll have nightmares tonight. A lager and a shot of that white lightning you make. God damn, I ran across a dead body at work today outside the dome, and it was someone I'd met a few times. The poor guy didn't have a suit on. Not just no suit, he wasn't wearing a stitch of clothing."

"Yeah, Ed here was telling me about it."

The mayor said "I hadn't heard that. They only said he had no suit."

The electrician asked "Ed, why isn't this in the news?"

"Beats me, but I'm holding a press conference about it tomorrow. Wilcox would have tried to keep it secret, but that's why he lost the election. Was it gruesome?"

Al downed his shot, took a sip of beer, and said "You wouldn't have wanted to be there. John, another shot, please. Make it a double.

Sam Woodside was a reporter for the Martian Times, one of several dozen such newspapers in Mars' many domes. Al Morton called him the next morning, a day after the discovery, with news of the dead body that he had found. The reporter asked the electrician "Who was he and how did he die?"

"I don't know. His first name was Bob, but I don't know what his last name was. He was an electrician, too, but he usually worked the other side of the dome from me and I didn't know him very well, I only met him a few times. His shop was short staffed so they assigned me on that side temporarily. You'll have to ask the cops his full name and how he died. I talked to the mayor last night at Hooker's, and they don't know much yet."

"Hookers?"

"Hooker's Tavern, named after a musician who lived in the nineteen hundreds. John Knolls is a good friend of mine and owns the place."

They spoke for another fifteen minutes without Sam learning much.

As he was beginning to dial the mayor's office to get more information, another call came in. It was from his boss, who assigned him to a press conference the mayor had scheduled for the morning.

Typical. He really wanted to write about the murder and here he had to attend a meaningless press conference. He wondered what it was about. "Probably something nobody would want to read about," he thought.

The news conference lasted a long time, even though little was yet known about the murder. The only clue had been the corpse itself, and it hadn't yet yielded any answers. They would have to wait for the coroner, who had possession of the case's only clue that had turned up so far.

The mayor issued an executive order that all airlocks be guarded, and that no one would be allowed outside the dome alone. Martians had to be extra cautious about everything, since the environment outside the domes was so deadly. Safety was drilled into native-born Martians from birth.

The mayor had of course been in contact with Dome Council members, all of whom were going to present a bill making the guards and the "nobody goes out alone" rule law. All had urged him to make the executive order, which would last until the council next met.

Sam wrote the story, which was on the front page with an extra large headline: "GRUESOME MURDER OUTSIDE THE DOME" and in smaller type, "Police Have Few Clues, No Suspects". Sam took what little information he had about the murder and skillfully stretched it to two full columns, most of which was the accounts of the electrician's grieving friends and family, and some of it slightly redundant.

The dome's police contacted a homicide investigator on Earth, who chided the Martian for doing so little investigating. "Come on, man, get a warrant and search the victim's home and workplace. It may have been for robbery, but there are a lot of things that cause murder. Find out who he associated with, if he was having any love affairs, who saw him last. Don't wait for the coroner! What did the crime scene look like?"

"Like there was a dust storm between when he was killed and when the body was found. If there were any footprints or wheel tracks or any other such evidence they were gone."

It seemed the newspaper had done more investigating than the police. The Martian took the Earthian policeman's advice, but still came up with little, at least at first.

"Hi, George, I was wondering if you were sick or something and didn't go to work today, you always drop by for a beer on your way home." John poured an ale for him.

"I ran really late tonight, somebody stole my tools. At first I thought somebody might have grabbed my tool box by mistake, but I'm pretty sure they were stolen. Anyway, I had to fill out a ton of paperwork for the insurance."

"Sorry to hear that, the tools must be expensive."

"Yeah, they are. Brand new tools, state of the art stuff. I was working on two panels around a corner from each other, and I had my tool chest by one panel when I was working on the other one. I closed that panel up and went to finish the side where my tools were, and they were gone.

"Like I was saying, at first I thought someone must have picked the tools up by mistake, but I noticed boot prints going away from the dome from where my tools had been. So when I got back in the dome and out of my suit I called the cops. I didn't think anyone picked them up by mistake after seeing footprints leading away from the dome. The cops said it was possible that were taken by mistake, but I don't think so. Talking to the cops took another hour."

A man in a policeman's uniform came in, sat down, and ordered a shot of Bourbon and a wheat beer. "Rough week," he told the bartender. "Murder a few days ago, probable theft today."

"Yeah, I heard."

The policeman looked at George. "Say, you're the fellow whose tools are missing, aren't you?"

George answered in the affirmative and ordered another beer. Obviously a little distraught, he had drunk the first one far faster than usual.

The officer said "those boot prints you saw led to wheel tracks. We followed them for ten kilometers, and it looked like a space craft had landed and taken off. We think pirates have your tools."

George shook his head sadly. "Damned pirates, the tools are insured but it'll take three weeks to get them replaced, and I won't be able to work."

"That sucks, George. Need to run a tab until your new tools come?" the bartender asked.

"Thanks, John, but I have enough cash and credit to make it until I can get new tools delivered."

The police officer finished his beer and shot and walked home, just as Mayor Waldo came in. "Hi, John. We had a theft today, give me the usual."

"Hi, Ed. Yeah, I heard," he said, pouring the mayor a beer and the thirsty electrician a third beer.

Ed sighed. "News travels fast."

John laughed. "Where would you go if your tools were stolen and you couldn't work for weeks? You know George, don't you?"

"Yeah, hi George. Those were your tools?"

"Yeah, it really sucks."

"Anything I can do? Or the dome can do?"

George laughed. "Yeah, get a better football team, the Australians and Europeans always kick our asses!"

Talk drifted off to sports for a while, and a thought came to John. "Ed," he said, "Could the pirates have committed that murder?"

"No, they would have taken him to their ship so they wouldn't harm the suit. Everyone knows how valuable a suit is. They would have just dumped the body in space."

"You ought to dump those footballers in space," George said dourly.

The mayor and bartender laughed, and talk went back to sports as more people started trickling in.

The next day the Chief of Police called the mayor with news of clues: the dead man's tools and environment suit were missing. Did someone murder him for his suit and tools? It looked like that was the motive, although police were still investigating the victim's associates. If they found that suit and those tools, they would likely find the murderer.

Things seemed to be looking up. He usually only stopped by John's bar when he'd had a bad day or a seemingly insoluble problem, but he decided to make an exception this time since his old friend Charlie Onehorse would be there. Charlie was the mayor of Dome Australia Two, about twenty kilometers from his dome. Old Charlie had been visiting on a trade mission.

When he got off work, John's bar was already filling up. "Ed!" came a voice from the gloom, as his eyes hadn't yet adjusted, but he knew that voice.

"Hey, Charlie! How did your deal go?"

"Ace, even though those blokes aren't drongos, but the deals always go well. Almost all of them, anyway. I heard your dome had a homicide?"

"Yeah, it sure looks like the poor guy was murdered. Had some thefts, too, but one of them looks like pirates."

"Maybe it was pirates that killed that bloke," Charlie said.

"That's what John said, but like I told him, they would have just carried him and his suit away and dumped the body in space."

"Yeah, you're right, they would have. Damned pirates, I hope they leave my dome alone. Hey, John, get a grog for Ed, would you?" Just then a robot rolled up with Mayor Waldo's beer.

At the other end of the bar, John was talking to Al. Al had been telling him of the nightmarishly horrible discovery and how it was affecting him for the last few days, which he had mostly spent in the bar getting very drunk. "Al, I want you to meet a friend of mine," John said as an attractive woman walked up. "Al, meet Tammy Winters."

"Hello, Ms. Winters."

"It's doctor, but call me Tammy. John tells me you're having some problems."

Al glared at John angrily. Tammy said "Look, Al, your reaction to what you've gone through is normal. Look, I have a friend who needs some new patients, could you help him out?" and handed him her colleague's business card.

"Well, I don't know," Al said, looking at the card. "What will it cost?"

"Nothing, the government pays for it."

"Thanks, I will!"

Tammy replied "John, are you going to pour me a beer or what?"

Several days later the coroner's report came back, right before the mayor was due to go home, and Mayor Waldo was puzzled. The report said the victim had a stroke; a blood vessel in his brain had burst and he'd died instantly. But why was he out there naked?

He decided to talk to John. John always had an answer when things got crazy.

"Holy crap," Sam said when he got the news. "Damn, the most sensational news in my career and it wasn't. How can I spin this? The boss wants more papers sold!"

He decided to focus on the mystery of the naked corpse.

"And your cops can't figure it out, either?" John asked.

"No," said Ed. "It's still a mystery."

"Christ, Ed, it's as plain as the nose on your face! Look, only a few days later George's tools were stolen, and the police say it was pirates. It's simple, Ed. They were waiting for a chance to steal the poor guy's expensive tools and he collapsed. So they not only stole his tools, but his environment suit and clothing as well. Why didn't you guys see that?"

Ed scratched his head. "I don't know, but it makes sense. I'll talk to the police chief about it tomorrow." Just then George entered.

"John!" he yelled. "Drinks for everybody! WOO HOO!"

"What happened?" Ed asked.

"John's army!"

"John's army?"

"It isn't my army," John said. "More Dewey's than anyone's, I only hold maybe fifteen percent of Green-Osbourne."

George said "I can't thank you enough, John."

"George, I didn't do anything, there wasn't anything I could do," John replied. "We capture pirates all the time. It earns us a lot of cash and makes shipping easier for everybody, including our competition. You just got lucky."

"I don't care, I'm still grateful. They said I'd have my tools back the day after tomorrow.

"Oh, and Ed—they found Bob's suit and tools when they found my tools."

John grinned. "See?"

After the Mayor's press conference the next morning, Sam cursed. How could he spin this one without looking like a damned fool?

Cornodium

I'm going to kill a planet. I don't know how yet, but I swear I'm going to do it.

I was making a routine prospecting run and got a radio message from my best friend. As luck and coincidence would have it, the radio relay was only a little over two light hours away—and Roger was either dying or already dead.

The radio's message started "Warning! Anyone who hears this, stay away from Darius. This is probably the deadliest planet in the galaxy. If you land here, you'll die here. I'll probably be dead by the time you receive this message."

Darius? He was prospecting in the Luhman system, the same system that I was, and I didn't even know it. I doubt he knew I was in the system, too. I hadn't heard from him in months, and here he was only between a light hour and three away. I wondered what he was looking for? I was after rare earths. This system was supposed to be a lot like the solar system and we'd mined quite a bit of it from our own asteroid belt. Most of the rare earths in the belt, in fact. But Darius? What of value could possibly be there?

I couldn't bring myself to leave him there despite his dire warnings, at least until I'd heard the entire thing and knew he was... Oh, God. Roger!

I started the jump drive and in half an hour I'd be on my way to Darius to see if there was any way I could help him survive. I listened to the rest of the message as the engines warmed up.

"I don't remember the crash, but I suspect it was the cornodium that caused it. Do not land on this planet!"

I wondered what in the galaxy cornodium was. I'd never heard of the stuff before.

"I woke up on the floor with a terrible headache, not knowing where I was. Hung over, maybe? I sat up and looked around. No, I was in the pilot room of my craft and wouldn't have been drinking. I got up with my head reeling, and stumbled to the controls.

"It looked like I'd crashed on Darius, the third orbit out from Luhman. That's the weirdest star system we've found so far, weird because it was so much like the sun, and its planets were so much like our own solar system's planets. Darius even has a giant satellite like Earth does, and the Luhman system even has a ring of asteroids between the fourth and fifth planets, just like the solar system. Nature is really strange sometimes.

"I was looking for cornodium. Only small amounts had been found anywhere, and my calculations said the substance would be here, and likely vast riches of it. I don't know how many of us prospectors roam the galaxy these days, but we've looked for valuable ores either not readily available or not available at all in our own system on hundreds of thousands of planets, and cornodium had only been found on six of them. None had much of it. It had all been mined and taken to Earth, less than a ton of the substance.

"I didn't know much about cornodium despite doing as much research as I could about it. It was discovered only ten years ago and had revolutionized high end electronics, and the highest end at that because the stuff was so rare, and therefore very expensive. All I knew about cornodium was that they used it for power generation, but I had no idea how they got power from it. I didn't know what the stuff is or why it's so rare, but I didn't care. All I knew was that it was rare and very expensive, and if I found a planet with it I'd be rich, so I learned as much about its origins as I could. I was sure Darius fit the bill. If I was right I'd be as rich as my buddy who had found all that gold and platinum. I know now. Lot of good it will do a dead man."

I choked up again; Roger was thinking of me as he died.

"Well, I would have been rich. It was obvious I'd crash landed on Darius.

"My head was bleeding, which explained the headache. I ignored it; I needed to assess my situation and get help if necessary.

"I checked the controls, and yep, I was screwed. I tried to radio for help, but radio only goes at the speed of light and the closest radio relay craft was thirty light minutes away. I sent a distress signal, knowing it would be over an hour before I heard back.

"Two hours later it dawned on me—the antenna was on the bottom of the craft to better communicate with bodies one was taking off from or landing on. No one had heard me.

"Like I said, Darius is really weird. They'd only surveyed it by telescope so far, but It's exactly like Earth and its moon, with two exceptions: the land masses are quite different, and there is no life whatever. The air is mostly nitrogen like Earth, with about the same amount of oxygen and carbon dioxide, and science couldn't explain where the oxygen came from. On Earth, it comes from vegetation and photosynthesis, but Darius was completely lifeless.

"That didn't matter to me, though. I needed to find the cornodium I was certain was here and stake a claim.

"The trouble was, I seemed to have wrecked my craft, and it was all I had. It was insured, of course, but with my antenna busted how could I collect on the insurance? And find the cornodium and stake a claim?

“I decided to go outside and think about it, since I needed to see how much damage was done in the crash. After all, what danger could there be? This planet was lifeless, including microbial life. It being lifeless was, of course, the biggest mystery, even bigger than where all the oxygen had all come from. The planet was perfect for life to have formed, yet it hadn’t. It should have even had sentient life, even though so far our own species was the only sentience we had ever found, which still puzzled evolutionists. We’d discovered lots of life in the galaxy, but most of it was no higher form of life than bacteria, and none smarter than a cow is on Earth.

“I got out to do an outside inspection, and wow, I was right; the bright blue cornodium was everywhere, just laying on the ground! One piece looked like a daisy; nature comes up with some strange coincidences, and I laughed at it. There was a weird sound in the air, and I couldn’t figure out what it was or where it was coming from.

“It looked like I’d smashed up the bottom of my craft pretty good. I’d have to find a way to make the radio work, and I decided to eat lunch and take a short walk first, since I was going to need all my brain and it didn’t seem to be working right, so I decided to give it a break. I ate lunch and went back outside.

“Darius reminded me of Mars, except there was air and water. And mud. And the sky’s blue when Luhman is shining. It wasn’t the same color as Mars, either, more brown than orange, with all of the patches of the bright blue cornodium. Lots of large areas didn’t show dirt, just piles of small to tiny pieces of cornodium. And that strange sound, and it was heavy like Earth and the horizon was different than Mars, but it still reminded me of Mars, anyway. I don’t know why.

“It wasn’t all that muddy, kind of like dry dirt that had a small shower maybe the day before and there were enough rocks to keep my boots from getting too nasty. Most of the rock and gravel was cornodium.

“I figured the planet wouldn’t be lifeless for long; this system had only been discovered six months ago. I came out as soon as I'd heard of it, because I had a hunch based on what I'd read about cornodium: it had only been found on lifeless planets with gravities between Mars' gravity and one point five Earth gravities within a star's "Goldilocks zone", and Darius fit perfectly. I wondered why nobody else had figured that out, the numbers were all there.

"I walked up a shallow incline, and when I reached the top I saw in the distance what looked like it might have been a large machine, halfway buried. I started walking toward it to investigate, but it started sprinkling and the sky looked menacing, so I went back to my ship. I needed to work on that radio, anyway. I'd have to find some wire that didn't feed the radio or kitchen or air refreshment to use as an antenna.

"Shortly after I was inside my craft it started storming badly, with thunder's noise and the wind's howl echoing through the boat constantly. I searched the ship for wire I could scavenge from the wreckage without stopping the kitchen or radio. I found enough to reach just outside, and now needed something to use as an antenna.

"I thought of what had looked like half-buried machinery, and hoped there was wire in it, since all I would need for an antenna was a little more wire. I figured to go exploring it as soon as the storm abated.

"It stormed all afternoon and half the night. The next morning when I woke up, Luhman was shining brightly in a cloudless sky. I ate breakfast, despite not being very hungry, and packed a lunch, because it had looked like the machine might be quite a way off. It seemed I'd gotten a concussion in the crash, because my head still hurt, and I was still weak and disoriented. My stomach was a bit queasy, too, especially after breakfast.

"It was a two hour walk to the machine, and I had to rest halfway there. Where was my normal stamina? I should have been able to sprint to it. 'Probably has to do with the concussion,' I thought. I still wasn't thinking clearly.

"The thing was bigger and farther away than it looked. Space ship, perhaps? I looked for a door or a window or a hatch. I didn't find one, but I did find an opening where the thing's metal had torn; it had to be some sort of craft, although it was nothing like any craft I'd ever seen or imagined.

"I didn't find any wire, but I did find a steel rod I could use for an antenna, and two statues of some weird animal I'd never heard of, clothed in rags and made of cornodium. There were strange sounds coming from the statues. Art? Or... A chill went up my spine. Were these intelligent aliens that had somehow become cornodium? I thought of when I'd seen what looked like a flower made of cornodium earlier, and had thought it was one of those coincidental freaks of nature.

"By then I wasn't feeling well at all. In fact I felt downright sick, and decided to go back to my boat. I went outside, and noticed that my skin had taken on a slightly bluish tint.

"By the time I got back I was weak and shaky, and cold. Really cold, as if I'd been in the snow in summer clothes, even though the day was very warm, almost hot. It only took a minute to hang the rod from the wire and start the radio.

"I had made quite a few incredibly profound discoveries, discoveries that were incredibly important to humanity. I'd found evidence of alien intelligent life in the crashed alien craft, and another alien was taking me over—the planet itself. Rather than being lifeless, the planet itself is alive. It grows, reproduces, and eats. The cornodium is its brain! I now know why the strange sounds were coming from the alien statues; the planet was trying to taunt me in an alien language. It's talking inside my head right now, in English. I... I have to... I have to set this on repeat... before Darius...

"Warning! Anyone who hears this, stay away from Darius. This is probably the deadliest planet in the galaxy. If you land here, you'll die here. I'll probably be..."

I shut it off and saved my best friend's last words, tears welling up in my eyes. Even if I could have gotten to him in time, I couldn't have rescued him. I doubt it's possible to land safely on Darius, as I suspect it caused Roger's craft to crash land.

The jump drive made it seem like I got to Darius immediately, but it would have actually been five to twenty minutes later when I really got there, and hours since he had sent the message. I went into orbit around Darius and called the survey bureau and staked a claim to it. Nobody's going to make batteries out of my friend! And I'm going to contact the authorities when I get to Earth and see if I can get the use of cornodium outlawed before all life there becomes cornodium. And I'm going to learn everything I can about the stuff. Including how to kill it.

God, but the government is exasperating! I not only didn't make any progress getting cornodium outlawed, I was issued a gag order! The substance promised to do wonders for the economy, because it seemed to produce free energy, despite the laws of thermodynamics.

But of course it wasn't doing that. It was getting energy from somewhere, and I was convinced that the somewhere was from the energy in life forms that were, little by little, becoming cornodium themselves. My friend Roger who had died and become cornodium died in a about a day, but it had been a planet that was almost completely covered in it. People, animals, and plants on Earth were only exposed to tiny amounts of it. They would die of old age before becoming cornodium, because there was so little of it.

But eventually Earth would become cornodium, I was sure. Ultimately enough live matter would become cornodium that it would awaken and eat everything that lived on Earth.

I'm a very wealthy person, having discovered a planet that was mostly made of gold and another made of mostly platinum, two metals that are incredibly useful in electronics, and my mining licenses don't come cheap. I decided to buy as much cornodium as I could, hopefully all of it, and send it to Darius. I hoped I could afford it.

I'd bought half a ton at ridiculous prices when the government stepped in again. I'd dropped all the cornodium on Darius, and they took Darius from me. Imminent domain. There were a year of legal battles but I lost. Sure, I made a fortune on it, and I was now the richest individual on Earth, but damn it, I wanted Earth to live and these idiots were going to kill it!

Crap. What to do next? I decided to chance ignoring the gag order and talk to a scientist, and contacted a local university. I was to have a meeting with a Dr. Felber, a materials scientist who was studying cornodium and trying to find a way to make artificial cornodium and a way to recharge cornodium batteries. I was a little uncertain about what the outcome might be, what with the gag order and all.

She turned out to be a delightful woman, but of course the court order had me worried. "Dr. Felber," I said, "I've been under a gag order about cornodium, and I'm not supposed to talk to anyone at all about it or they'll put me in prison. Can you keep this to yourself?"

She became a bit pensive. "Not if it's something subversive."

"It isn't. I have a recording of a dead friend that I'm not allowed to play anywhere, and if they knew it existed it wouldn't exist. They had erased it from the radio relay's data banks, but didn't know I'd kept a copy."

She raised an eyebrow. "Play it," she said. I did.

When it was finished, she said "I've been exposed."

"Yes," I replied, "and so have I. But there is so little of it you'll be dead of old age long before it affects the tissues; Roger was on a planet where most of the whole crust was covered in cornodium. But we need to save the Earth!"

"Yes," she agreed, "But how?"

"I don't know, you're the scientist. How can we kill it?"

"Kill what?" she asked.

"Kill Darius," I said vengefully.

"Kill a planet?"

"Yes," I replied, "before it kills us! It will, you know, if it lives."

She looked doubtful. "I'm going to have to study that sample some more, our present theories may all be wrong. That recording explains a few things that had puzzled us and may be a paradigm changer. I'll get back to you. Don't worry, this is between us."

A year and a half later rumors started leaking about government mining expeditions that had gone to Darius, all of whom had "mysteriously" disappeared. It was no mystery to me; those people were now all cornodium, no longer human, or even alive as we know life. They had been eaten by the evil monster that was Darius.

Friends and relatives of the missing people were served the same gag order that I had been served, and a few were jailed after publicly complaining. So far, it was only rumor as far as the public was concerned... for now. Later on, a lot of politicians lost their jobs. But I'm getting ahead of myself.

Six months after the rumors started, Dr. Felber emailed me. "See what I found" is all the email said. So I did, and visited her at the university.

"It's easy to kill," she said when I visited her. "Middle C."

"Middle C?" I asked, perplexed.

"Two hundred sixty one point six Hertz," she replied. "That tone kills it. Earth is full of music, including that note, which we think is why they ever run down at all, so we have nothing to worry about."

My jaw dropped. "So if Roger had been playing music there he wouldn't have died?"

"Maybe, maybe not. It might have taken a very loud continuously operating tone generator, and even that might not have been enough.

"There are only tiny amounts in any one place on Earth, where there's lots of music, and cornodium batteries last ten years or more, and most of Darius is covered in the stuff.

"In any case, even if he had lived, the cornodium would have been useless. Like the Land Bridge theory was replaced by continental drift, and the solid state universe was discarded in favor of the big bang theory, all of our theories about what made it vibrate were completely wrong.

"We had believed that the vibration was caused by some process internal to the substance and trying to find where its power was stored; we had thought it must have been a chemical reaction that we hadn't found. It made perfectly logical sense, since it seemed that the energy drained like a normal old fashioned chemical battery, except far more slowly and they couldn't be recharged. People have been seriously injured trying to recharge them."

Wow. Dead cornodium wasn't useless. I wondered why nobody thought of military and construction applications, since such a small amount was so explosive; the cornodium in a two thousand watt battery was only about a cubic centimeter in size, although most of the battery is the piezoelectrics and the battery takes up a lot more room than a cubic centimeter, more like four cubic decimeters, and that two thousand watts lasts for ten years or more. Yes, I'd learned a lot about cornodium since Darius had murdered Roger.

Of course I didn't say anything; kept to myself this could bankroll whatever it took to kill Darius. I needed to get that planet back.

And kill the evil thing and let the military and construction crews blow the stuff up. Roger didn't deserve to die like that! I'd had my legal team negotiating with the government for months by then, ever since the rumors about the missing miners had started floating around.

Six months later the government, failing to find a way to mine Darius, ceded the planet's rights back to me, at twenty percent of what they'd paid me for it. Of course there were a lot of lawyers involved, but I can afford the best, and you can trust that I hired the best. When you need a lawyer, the most expensive one you can afford is usually your wisest investment.

The next day I was in orbit around Darius with a drone, a tone generator tuned to middle C, and a hamster. I would have used a plant, but didn't know how long it took for plant tissue to become cornodium, but it takes about a day with a mammal on Darius. I sent the drone down, wondering if it would crash.

It didn't, so the cornodium had affected Roger before he even landed. If he'd landed on autopilot the fool might have lived. But probably not.

This was a truly evil thing, and I planned to destroy it, full of hate for my friend's tormentor and executioner. Hate for the monster that had eaten him. Hate for the evil that wanted to consume all life.

Forty eight hours later the drone returned, with a cornodium statue of a hamster. Damn, the doctor was wrong. Oh, well, my cornodium hamster would pay for the trip and a whole lot more. That was a valuable statue, at least after it was made into batteries.

It was a six month jump from Luhman to Sol, and I don't understand the math behind that at all. The jump seemed instantaneous to me, but it was six months later when I arrived. The part I don't understand is it should have been years instead of months, and a whole lot more than only six. I simply don't understand jump drives. Yeah, they covered them in pilot school, but I just didn't get it. It has something to do with artificial worms drilling holes or something, and has a lot of really complicated math that has to do with space, time, and gravity. Like I said, it's over my head. I'm lucky I passed the test, it was multiple choice and I guessed at a lot of it.

In any case, when I got back to Earth I of course visited Dr. Felber, who told me "We have additional data since you left. The sonic frequency must be out of phase to discharge the cornodium; if it's in phase it strengthens it. It's still dangerous to Earth!"

"Have you said anything to anyone else?" I asked. "Please don't let anyone know cornodium batteries are rechargeable! My God..."

"Well, finding a way to recharge them was one of my original goals, but don't worry. This thing needs to be gone before we are. I'm working with an engineer on a device that will take the cornodium's frequency and send it back out of phase. I'll email you when it's done."

It only took a month and I was on my way back to Darius with my drone and another hamster. Again the generator was sounding middle C, but the computers had measured and sent a perfectly out of phase middle C. I waited the two days to see if it would come back a hamster or a cornodium statue of a hamster.

I got my hamster back, alive and bewildered. But maybe hamsters are always bewildered, I don't know. Anyway, it worked. I could mine explosives to make up for my losses now, then figure out how to kill this horrible thing once and for all. By "this horrible thing" I mean the monster, Darius, of course. That bitch has to die! I returned to Earth to talk to Dr. Felber again, and maybe talk to my government contacts whom I had sought out during and after the gag order and imminent domain court proceedings, about sales of explosives to them. It would depend on what Dr. Felber said.

Dr. Felber was pleased that the experiment was a success. "Add more amplifiers," she said, "then blow up the dead parts."

Blow up the dead parts? Not me, I was going to mine it and sell it to the government like a patriot and let them blow it up. But I took her advice on the amplification.

But first I needed to do one more experiment before talking to my government contacts, to see how much of Darius died from the out of phase middle C. I had one constructed that would run for two days then attempt to "recharge" it with electricity. According to Dr. Felber's theories, it should explode several square kilometers of the planet's surface.

It didn't. So she had some calculating to do, I guessed. I sent a drone down to collect a hamster-sized chunk of dead cornodium for her to examine.

I jumped, and six months later even though it seemed like a second later I was in orbit around Earth, and talking to Dr. Felber again the next day. "It should have worked," she said. "Puzzling. We'll examine the sample you brought back and call when we have an answer."

"Okay," I said.

I waited in the Bahamas on a beach. No point stressing about it, we'd kill that terrible thing eventually.

I sat on that beach for months. Finally Dr. Felber contacted me. "It has to be processed before it's explosive," she said.

"Processed?" I had no idea how these batteries worked, even though I'd tried to learn. It did make me think of something Roger said in his warning—it had stormed when he was there. If raw cornodium had been explosive it would have blown him up.

"Ground into a fine powder. Do that and the individual grains all sing in harmony, and you can turn that into a lot of electricity with a piezoelectric device, a really small one. Here, I'll show you the math..."

"Don't bother," I interrupted, "I wouldn't understand it anyway."

"Well, okay," she said, "but we can still kill Darius if you can afford it."

"I can afford it," I said. "How?"

"It emits sound. Kill a patch with your biggest amplifier and send a robot with a sound meter tuned to middle C to see how much is dead, and you can kill Darius a little at a time."

"Yes!" I exclaimed. "Let that bastard suffer!" God, but I hated Darius because of poor Roger, who had been killed with extreme malice. It had to have been horrible for him.

I teared up a little. It seemed I wasn't going to sell anything to the government, since dead, unprocessed cornodium was worthless. But that wasn't what made me tear up, I was thinking of poor Roger. I missed my old buddy terribly. We were partners way back when these boats needed two people to fly them, and still got together all these long years later. We had some great times, and I was looking forward to more good times. But it was too late now.

The next day I made the jump to Darius with a huge bank of midrange speakers, a phased C tone generator, and fifty thousand watts of amplification, with all of it mobile. I sent a robot with a sound meter down with them.

The next day the robot reported a dead zone a hundred meters wide, so I sent all the equipment moving in an ever widening spiral. When this land mass was clean I'd move it all to another land mass and get to work there. I figured it would take months to kill the entire planet, but I was determined.

A week later the spiral, now a hundred kilometer radius, wasn't widening. Apparently, dead cornodium could regenerate in the presence of live cornodium. I left the equipment there running in circles, not wanting my meager progress to be erased, and went back to Earth for more sound equipment. Before I left I had a drone land with a robot to collect a few hundred kilos of live cornodium to bankroll the venture with.

Killing Darius would be worth the incredible riches I was going to destroy by killing it. Poor Roger!

I got to Earth immediately six months later. I sold the cornodium, mostly to Chinese buyers, and bought a huge number of mobile amplifiers, speakers, and the computerized gizmos that sent cornodium's middle C signature back out of phase. I also bought the nicest casket I could find for Roger, and hired an engineer. An expensive one who had several different engineering degrees.

I worried about taking all that cornodium to Earth, but the newspapers said that there was a backlash against cornodium and the rich people who used it, and middle C phase generators were becoming popular among normal folks who couldn't afford cornodium devices and were afraid of them. Justifiably afraid, I thought, despite Dr. Felber's initial reassurances. That relieved me quite a bit.

I thought it was funny, I was very wealthy and rather than using cornodium devices, I was the first to call for their prohibition. But I did have more cornodium than anyone, a whole planet full, even though I was extirpating all of it. Well, what I didn't sell, mostly to China, at least.

A year later, Darius seemed completely dead. There wasn't a milligram of cornodium on any of the land masses at all, even dead cornodium; I'd mined it all and sent it to the heart of the perpetual fusion explosion known as Luhman.

It looked like Darius had destroyed an intelligent species from what few artifacts had surfaced. The planet had been lifeless for a long, long time and very little was left to tell us about these aliens, but this monster had very obviously destroyed a great spacefaring civilization.

Of course, before mining the dead cornodium and sending it to the star we recovered the cornodium bodies of the people who had tried to mine cornodium for the government, Darian artifacts (We found a cornodium Darian, but we don't know if it was the intelligent species), and the intelligent aliens Roger found that Darius had eaten, and shipped them to Earth. The bodies, both alien and human, were now dead cornodium and therefore harmless as long as they were kept away from live cornodium. The few ruins of stone buildings stayed, as did Roger's ship and the alien ship. Maybe some day they would be tourist attractions.

I thought I had beaten the evil monster, but I hadn't.

I had several tons of Earthian dirt shipped to Darius for its microbes, and enough grass seed to wipe out the supplier's inventory. I was determined to bring Earthian life to Darius, starting with grass and then with cows, and other species of flora and fauna later. I had a home by the sea side built there, and a shrine and burial site for Roger. I really missed Roger and the good times we'd had together.

I ran the C generator for a year just in case, with nary a peep from it, and finally shut it off. I shouldn't have.

I went back to Earth for a visit, and to buy supplies. The few folks I had hired took care of my grass and cows when I was gone. Those cows were incredibly useful, widening the zone where plants would grow.

Back on Earth, the Chinese had really taken to cornodium batteries. They actually believed that the batteries promoted health! Very wealthy Chinese folks powered their entire households with cornodium batteries. The government there had outlawed phased C generators, saying they were a plot to ruin the Chinese economy.

However, in the Americas, particularly South America, most communities had outlawed cornodium. It was illegal in all of Peru and Venezuela, as well as most communities in the rest of the countries in those continents. It was also illegal in much of New Zealand, Australia, and in parts of many African and Asian nations. Europe was in the grip of a massive economic recession, so there were very few cornodium devices there. Most of the world got power from rooftop solar panels and back yard windmills. China was the only country still using fossil fuels, and was the only country to outlaw the phased C devices.

They had also developed something called "twist jump radio". I don't understand how it works, but it has something to do with "twisted pairs of photons". At any rate, it made communication instantaneous no matter how far away the other radio was... well, usually. Sometimes there were lags, and the theoretical physicists were still trying to figure out why.

This was a real breakthrough in communications, since normal radio was useless between stellar systems, and messages had to be sent physically on a ship with jump drive.

Of course, I bought five of them.

After visiting friends and family I returned to Darius with all sorts of seeds, several honeybee hives, some pigs, chickens, a few other animals, my new twisted radios, and other supplies. Darius would become a pest-free paradise.

A few months later I made the mistake of wading in the ocean for an hour or two, maybe even longer. It made me weak and dizzy and nauseous and I had a terrible headache, so I headed back to the house. I noticed that my skin seemed to have a slight blue tint, as if I were really cold, and I felt like I was freezing.

On a hunch I turned the C generator on, and it came on very loud; there was cornodium somewhere, and lots of it.

The cornodium it was reacting to was in me! I was suffering from cornodium poisoning, the same thing that had killed Roger.

The ocean... I'd forgotten about aquatic life, and apparently the seas, rivers, and lakes were full of that damned cornodium. I got a blanket and sat weakly on a recliner, hoping the C generator would help.

It did. An hour later my chills became a fever, and I threw up my breakfast. The vomit was blue, and later my urine and feces were blue as well. I was perspiring profusely, and my sweat came out with a blueish tint. I couldn't eat at all for a week, and it was a sick, painful, miserable month before I was anywhere near normal.

When I was mostly over the poisoning I returned to Earth again to hire another engineer to help me figure out how to kill the rest of Darius and to talk to Dr. Felber about sending an out of phase signal underwater. It turned out that she knew little about underwater sound, but put me in touch with a sonic engineer who could, and he got me acquainted with another engineer who specialized in robotic submarines. Both agreed to visit Darius and work on the underwater sonic equipment.

The news on Earth was all about a panic in China, and it was about cornodium. It seems that a large part of the very wealthy Zhejiang Provence had succumbed to cornodium poisoning, and thousands of people and uncounted plants and animals there were now cornodium. The Chinese government quickly outlawed cornodium and cordoned the area with phased C generators. They then confiscated every cornodium device in China and sent them to the sun, and suspended trade with any country where cornodium was legal.

The engineers and about fifty other folks went to Darius with me and a great big load of supplies, as I had more and more people working for me on Darius now. It wouldn't be long before Darius was self-sufficient, at least as far as food was concerned. We'd need to import some robotic harvesters soon.

Everyone wore a C generator on their belts to protect against cornodium poisoning, and we put up large phased C generators every hundred meters along all the planet's seashores.

Of course, one of the workers, new to Darius, got drunk and fell into the ocean. His two drunken buddies hauled him out laughing, and took him home. They weren't laughing for long, though, as all three developed mild cases of cornodium poisoning. Even a "mild" case is pure sick and painful misery, but at least now we knew that a C generator was a cure.

A message came over the twist radio from a doctor on Earth saying that one of the men had gotten a routine physical before coming to Darius, and his test results showed that he had developed a small tumor in one of his lungs and had to return to Earth for treatment immediately. It was the man who had drunkenly fallen into the water. The message had been terribly lagged, and should have reached Darius months before we did.

The engineers, both family men, went back to their families on Earth. I accompanied the three of them, deciding to get a physical myself; I hadn't seen a doctor in years and actually worried a little about the cornodium's effect on my health after I found out about the guy's tumor. After all, who knows? The stuff might cause cancer or something later.

The doctor said she was amazed at my health. I was almost fifty, and she said I looked thirty five and my vitals were normal for a healthy twenty five year old!

She'd been the doctor I'd seen years earlier, and asked when I'd had my mole removed and who had done the surgery.

"I didn't," I said. "I hadn't noticed it was missing."

"Puzzling," she said. "They don't usually go away by themselves. Your vitals are puzzling, as well. I've never seen anyone your age so healthy."

After I left, the fellow with lung cancer whose name I can't remember called, saying he was going back to Darius with me.

"But you need cancer treatment," I exclaimed.

"Nope, the doc said he couldn't understand it, but there wasn't any cancer. Said none of my vitals were anything like they were when I saw him seven months ago either, said I was healthy as a twenty year old. My warts went away, too!"

I called Dr. Felber and told her what had happened, that it looked like controlled cornodium poisoning could cure some diseases. "Well, I don't know," she said, "a sample size of two isn't very meaningful. I'll talk to some of my colleagues."

When I got back to Darius I stopped decontamination of one medium sized lake. After all, if this was a cure for cancer...

Five months later Dr. Felber showed up with over a hundred other scientists, from different fields; biochemists, chemists, biologists, materials scientists like her, and a lot more.

One of the scientists was dying of liver cancer, contracted because of exposure to some chemical when he was young. He ran straight into the lake as soon as he left the ship!

None of my crewpeople went into the water to drag him out, since they'd seen how nasty even a mild case of cornodium poisoning was. However, after quite a while two dumbass PhDs waded in and got him out. They all got sick, of course. The scientist with the cancer almost died, I think. He was in the water a long time before his fellow scientists even missed him, and the cancer had weakened him considerably.

He did recover, though, and there was no cancer afterward. Three out of three!

A year later Dr. Felber published her team's first report. Cornodium attacked the simplest life, like viruses, first. Next was microbial life, then aberrant cells in the higher life form, then that life form's healthy cells. It affected plants far more slowly than animals.

We'd not just cured cancer, but almost all diseases. It wouldn't cure diabetes, or arthritis, or baldness, or disease caused by genetics, or mental illnesses, but there were other treatments and cures for those ailments. It would cure the common cold or flu, but the cure was far worse than the disease in those cases. Believe me, you have to be really sick or dying before you'll want to get cornodium poising, even a mild case.

So we're building a health facility around that lake, and decontamination of the rest of the aquatic bodies continues, as does the research. Right now the biologists are testing its effects on heart disease in rodents, since the worry is that the cornodium may make it worse rather than better, we'll see.

Roger and I were hailed as heroes, saviors of the Earth. He hadn't died in vain after all.

I do worry, though. What if there's another cornodium planet somewhere?

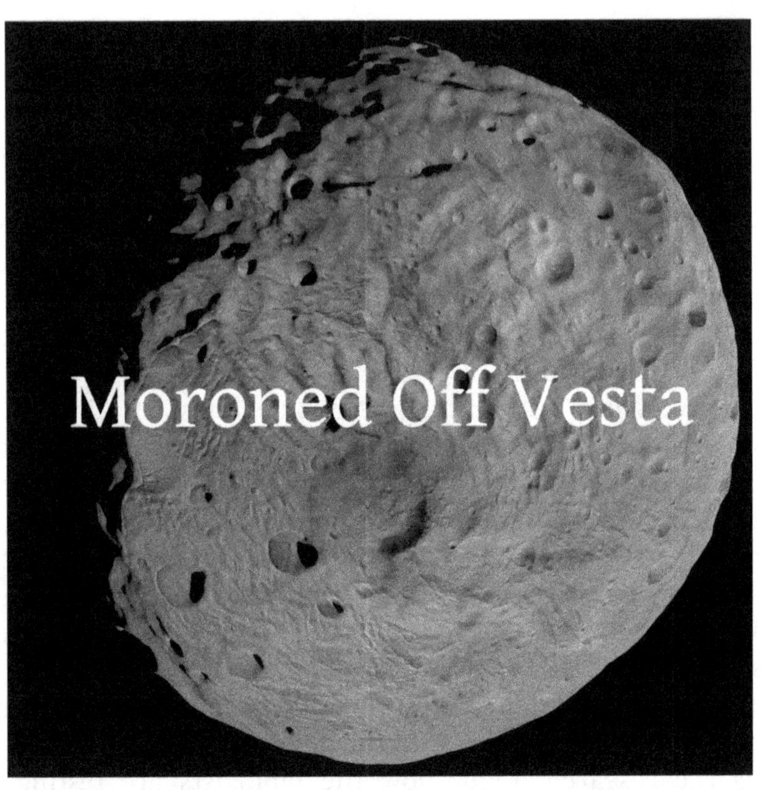

Moroned Off Vesta

John's first patron of the day was waiting at the door when he approached.

"Roger!" he said as he unlocked the door. "I haven't seen you in years! Want a beer? My stuff is pretty damned good if I do say so myself, and it's a lot cheaper than the imported stuff."

"Sure," Roger replied. John poured a beer and handed it to him. He took a sip. "Not bad, John. So you're tending bar now? I heard the shipping company fired you for that thing on Vesta. They said you killed a couple of guys."

John laughed. "Tending bar? It's my bar! Fired me? The president and the CEO both tried to talk me out of retiring, but my wife's building a telescope here. Time for me to settle down, I'm tired of pirates and all that other bullshit."

"Yeah, I heard you married a scientist. There hasn't been much pirate activity lately."

"Great! So what have you been up to, Rog?"

Roger laughed. "Well, I've been waiting for you to open for an hour most lately, it's been almost a year since I had a beer. I've had a bunch of Saturn runs and a Vesta assignment the last couple of years and haven't been to Mars in a long time, but when I got back from Vesta they sent me here with a load of barley and hops and stuff like that. Did you buy all of that?"

"Yeah, that's my shipment. I told you I'm making beer, didn't you see the sign? I have a microbrewery here, that's all beer ingredients. So how do you like it?"

"It's good beer, you're pretty good at it. So they begged you not to retire? When I was on Vesta unloading some food supplies they told me that you got fired for killing two passengers. Did that happen?"

John laughed. "No, not only did they not fire me, I got a raise. And yeah, two stupid rich tourists died but it was their own stupidity, arrogance, and sense of entitlement killed them, not me."

"So what happened?"

"Well, I was taking scientific equipment to Vesta and a couple of the other asteroid stations in the belt, and I had two first class passengers. A couple of assholes from Austin who were born rich and got richer speculating on the stock market. Idiots who couldn't learn because they thought they knew everything."

"Yeah," Roger said, "Texas is damned weird, I lived in Houston for a while when I was a kid. Everybody wore those stupid looking hats and acted like they were all ranchers or something. History class was filled with Sam Houston, the Alamo, and the Jet Propulsion Laboratory. It's been a museum for a couple hundred years now."

"Yeah, that's those two morons to a tee. Drug store cowboys, all hat and no cattle. Probably couldn't tell a cow from a horse and thought milk came from factories.

"All they did was bitch and complain and break rules. They hated the coffee I made for them, and my coffee's pretty good, lots better than robots did then. I'm glad they upgraded those robots, I always made coffee for passengers because the robot coffee was barely drinkable.

"They complained about the pork, too. What would I know about pork? Hell, I wasn't rich, I was just a boat captain. I only ate pork a couple of times in my life before I met Destiny. There wasn't anything I could have done about the pork but they bitched about it every damned day even though the cookbots did damned good on everything else but barbecue. Oh, they complained their asses off about the barbecue, too."

"They're crazy about barbecue in Texas," Roger said. "Some folks there eat it every day. I've seen them barbecue eggs! They're always bragging about how big everything is in Texas, too."

"Yeah, they bitched about how 'dinky' their cabin was. Hell, my whole damned houseboat would probably have fit in their living room and it's a big houseboat. Crappy trip, the only good thing was they were paying for full gravity so it didn't take very long to get there.

"Anyway, these guys liked reading old science fiction, really ancient stuff. They'd run across a short story called *Marooned Off Vesta,* and when Vesta ordered supplies from one of their companies they decided to buy tickets and ride along.

"These dumbasses wanted to recreate the damned story!"

"What was the story about?"

"Well, it starts with..." Another patron entered. "Gus Harrison! How about that!" John said.

Roger grinned. "What are you doing in a bar this time of morning, old man? I haven't seen you in years, either."

Gus laughed. "You're the one with a beer in front of you. I just got back from Europa and haven't had a beer in months. What do you have, John?"

"Pretty much everything, but my best seller is my own stuff."

"John makes some damned good beer," Roger said. "I like it better than imported. Give me another one, John."

"Yeah, I'll try one," said Gus. "So what have you guys been doing?"

"John's been telling space stories. He was telling me about some morons off Vesta."

"Yeah, like I was telling Roger, two annoying rich tourists wanted to recreate an ancient story some Russian guy wrote a few hundred years ago. It starts with three guys who have just survived a collision with an asteroid that destroyed most of the ship and killed everyone else."

"I think I read that," Gus said. "*Marooned Off Vesta?*"

"Yeah, that's the one."

"He wasn't Russian, he was American, Isaac Asimov. He emigrated to the United States with his parents from Russia when he was three. Rog, in the book one of the three guys puts on a space suit, crawls around the outside of the ship and blasts the ship's water tank with a laser or something and the water shoots out and puts them on Vesta where they're rescued by its science station. So what happened on your trip, John?"

"Well, these morons thought the guys in the story could have just jumped from orbit and landed on Vesta and decided to prove it."

"What?" Gus and Roger exclaimed in unison.

"That's just stupid," Gus added.

"No shit," John replied. "Well, they found out the hard way."

"How did they get outside the boat?" Roger asked. "We keep everything like storage locked away from passengers."

"They hacked the lock with some kind of gizmo they bought on the black market. It was really damned sophisticated, it kept the alarm quiet and the warning light dark."

"Son of a bitch," Gus said, "The stupid bastards dealt with pirates? They're lucky they lived long enough to buy the tickets. So they suffocated out there after they ran out of air?"

"No, worse. It was bad. I discovered it half an hour after they were floating outside and the meteor alarm went off. Lucky they wasn't able to unhook that alarm, or it really would have been like that story, only we'd all have died. There wasn't time to rescue the morons so I got the hell out of the way of the rocks. When the storm passed I went back into orbit and retrieved what little of them that was left, and delivered the cargo and the dead morons to the landing boat from the station."

"Almost wrecked your ship, did they?" Roger said.

"Yeah. I was moroned off Vesta."

The Exhibit

The entire universe was turned inside out and upside down and completely backwards today, and I must have been the only one to see it. It all started with an innocent looking email.

I get a lot of emails like this one, except that the note's subject line looked like a headline from the *National Enquirer*, or maybe *The Onion*. It read "Archaeologists Find Twenty Five Million Year Old iPhone." Misaddressed, maybe? But it was a press release for an art exhibit.

A few minutes after I set the mail aside is when it hit me; the fellow who sent the email had mentioned that he'd seen my work before and knew I'd written about art and wanted me to see his exhibit. I had written a story, *one* story, ten years earlier, and the paper hadn't published it.

I printed it out and went to see Frank, my boss.

"What's up, Stan?" he asked.

"I just got the strangest email" I said, handing him the printout. He read it.

"So what's so weird, Stan? You must get these every day!"

"What's weird is that yeah, I'm working on that story about the city museum, but I haven't even finished researching it and barely have an outline, and I only wrote one other art thing, and it was never published!"

"Huh, that is weird. Why don't you go down and check the place out?"

"You know, Frank, I think I will. Maybe I'll get a fun story out of it."

It was here in town, 568 Broadway, up in the eleventh floor. It was only about a fifteen minutes ride on the subway, and I rode the elevator up.

It looked like an Apple store, only it was as weird as the email. For instance, it had strange iPhone accessories, like a case with a built-in hourglass. It was like an Apple store in some twisted alternate dimension.

I had expected to see Evan Yee, the artist behind the installation, but nobody was there at all. Also weird. I took a few photos and left, disappointed that I had gotten no story out of it.

I went to the elevator, and there was no elevator. Instead, there was a door leading outside, at street level. I wondered if I was going crazy, and remembered the time my mother said she had a "senior moment". Maybe I was just getting old, but I was only forty five.

I reached for my phone as I walked outside, thinking that maybe I'd get some sort of inspiration from the pictures, but it was gone. Damn, that phone cost six hundred dollars! I was glad I'd noticed so soon, and turned around to go in—and it was an Apple store. Between losing my phone and my disorientation when I left the exhibit, I hadn't noticed that there hadn't been anyone outside.

By now I was sure I was going crazy. I went in anyway, and there was my phone, laying on one of the counters. I picked it up, looked around, and the place looked nothing like it had before I'd left, although it still looked like a weird, twisted, dystopian Apple store.

I left again, and the street and sidewalk were bright green. I just stood there a minute, kind of dazed, I guess. By then I was pretty sure I'd gone stark raving mad. Maybe I was having a stroke? I reached in my pocket to call for an ambulance, and my phone was gone. I could have sworn I'd stuck it in my pocket.

I went back in, and it wasn't an Apple store any more, just an empty room with my phone laying on the floor. I picked it up and tried to call 911, but there was no signal. I went outside again to get a signal; lots of buildings suck for phones, and it was now night; it had been morning when I'd gone in.

And there were two moons. Everything else was normal, but there were two moons in the sky and there were no people.

And my phone was missing again! Next phone I buy is going to be a cheap one. I went back inside, and it was an Apple store again, this time like any other Apple store. Again there was no one there, and again my phone was on the counter. And again, I could get no signal. I firmly gripped it in my fist and walked outside...

And confronted a monster! A giant animal, really huge, bigger than an elephant, with huge teeth and claws and feathers. I screamed and ran back inside... a cave.

And I'd dropped my phone outside in my fright. Not that it seemed to work any more, anyway. Or that it mattered, since I had clearly gone insane.

But I couldn't just sit in the cave. I waited a long time to make sure the monster was gone, then peeked outside. No monsters, and no phone. I went back in, I don't know why, and there was my phone laying on a large rock. I put it in my pocket, and noticed the cave had changed. It was huge before, now little more than an indentation in the rock face.

I went back out, and it looked like New York in the early twentieth century, except there were no people. I hadn't seen a soul since I'd started this ordeal, except for the monster.

And my phone was gone again. I turned around, and the Apple store's sign read "Bell Telephone". I went inside and there was a bank of antique switchboards, all unmanned. My phone was laying on one.

I put it back in my pocket and walked back out. I don't think I've ever been as worried and scared in my life, especially when I'd seen the huge, weird looking animal. This time the streets and signs of civilization were gone, and a group of wigwams was there where New York City had been before.

I was shaking. I sat down on a log, put my face in my hands and cried like a baby. I felt like one, lost like no lost child had ever been lost before.

Cried out, I sat and tried to think of a way out of the mess I'd somehow gotten myself into. The only thing I could think of was going back into the wigwam.

There was a room filled with some very strange looking machinery, machinery I'd never seen before and had an idea that no one else had either. And there were people there this time! Two women, a blonde and a brunette, both wearing extremely strange looking clothing, intently poring over a complex-looking gizmo that looked like it was from some science fiction movie, and didn't notice my entry. I stood there speechless.

"We almost had him!" one of the women exclaimed. "In the right dimension and we almost had him in the right time. It would have taken only one more minute. If he'd just sat still a little longer!"

"I can't find when he is now. This thing is being extra finicky today," the other woman remarked.

"Excuse me," I said, "But would someone please call 911? I think I've had a stroke or something."

They both whirled around at the same time. The blonde said "Oh, no, he's now!"

The brunette said "It will be all right, sir. Please, take your phone and wait in the hallway until it rings. There's a comfortable chair out there."

"What's going on?" I asked.

The blonde said "I'm sorry, we can't say anything more without fouling things up even worse than they already are. Please, your world will be normal in a few minutes, just listen for your phone."

"Uh, okay, I guess," I said, and took my phone outside and sat down.

Maybe fifteen minutes later I heard my ring tone, and it was coming from inside the office. I looked in my pocket and my phone was gone again.

I wondered if someone at work could have spiked my coffee with some hallucinogen, but no... nobody at the office would have done such a thing. I sighed, wondering what strangeness I was going to see next, and went in.

I was back at the art exhibit, and again, no one was there. I picked up the phone to answer it, but all that came out of it were some strange noises. I hung up, and I was getting a signal again! I called my boss.

"Where have you been?" Frank asked.

"I got lost. I may have had a stroke or something, I'm going to the doctor to get checked out. I'll call when I'm done to let you know."

"Well, I hope you're all right. I'll talk to you later."

"Bye."

I walked hesitantly out into the hallway, and the chair and door to the outside the building were gone, with the elevators taking their place. I pushed the button, and when the car came I stepped in gingerly, wondering what would happen when I got outside.

Outside the building everything seemed normal again, with the throngs of people and noise of vehicular traffic. I hailed a cab and took the taxi to the hospital, where they took my vitals and did a brain scan and some psychological tests. The doctor said everything looked normal, but my blood pressure was a little high and I should make an appointment with my regular doctor.

I took the subway back to the office. As I waited for the elevator, Doris, an editor, walked up—and she had red hair. Oh, no, I thought. "Your hair!" I said, scared again.

"Like it?" she said. "I was tired of being a blonde so I dyed it last night."

I could have hugged her. We took the elevator up and I went to see Frank.

"Frank, do you mind having someone else check out that exhibit? I don't think I could give them a fair revue."

Frank said I looked really pale and should go home, so I went home early. I couldn't get this weird day out of my mind, so I just wrote it down.

Of course, I'm not putting this in the paper. Maybe I'll send it to a science fiction magazine under an assumed name, because there's no way anyone could believe it wasn't fiction.

But I'm getting a new phone tomorrow.

"Say, Ed! How was your trip? Lager?"

"Hi, John. Yeah, I'll have a lager. The whole trip was lousy, a journey through hell all the way."

"Didn't you fly Green-Osbourne?"

"Well, yeah."

The bartender swore; he was a wealthy man who owned the bar he was tending and quite a bit of Green-Osbourne Transportation Company stock as well. "What went wrong on the trip?"

"Those stupid talking robots. God but I hate those things."

The bartender laughed. "Everybody does."

"Why do you have them talking, then?"

"Advertising and engineering want to point out our superior technology, including AI."

"Well, it's too much A and not much I at all. Those things are *really* stupid."

John snickered. He hated talking robots, too, but had been voted down at board meetings. The tendbot he used when it got too busy for a single bartender to easily handle he'd special ordered, with no voice, only screen printouts and beeps. Most people thought talking robots were creepy.

"Well, look, Ed, they can't really think. Programmers just use humans' built-in anthropomorphism and animism. It's a parlor trick, one of our engineers explained it to me once. So what did the stupid thing do?"

"It was dinner time, the first night of the trip. I'd bought a business class ticket and somehow wound up on a first class flight... Say, did you have something to do with that?"

John just smiled. "Go on, Ed, what did the stupid robot do?"

Ed gave John a funny look and continued. "Well, I'd never had pork before. I thought it must be extra tasty, considering how ridiculously expensive it is."

"Well, it's environmental regulations."

"Huh?"

"Sure, it's why Earth buys all its ores from space miners. Mining is pretty much illegal on Earth, because poisonous pollution from mining, farming, industry, and transportation nearly ruined the Earth's ability to sustain life a couple of centuries ago. It... Oh wow. Want to get rich, Ed?"

"Not particularly, why?"

"Someone will. We should build hog domes and farm pigs in them, and sell the pork to Earthians. I'd do it but I'm way too busy, what with Green-Osbourne, the bar, the brewery, and the farm I grow beer ingredients in."

"Well, I'll talk to a few folks. It would help Mars' economy. Fill me up, John," he said, sliding his glass across the bar. "Uh, what were we talking about?"

"Pork and robots."

"Huh?"

"Your trip."

"Oh, yeah, pork. Why is it so expensive?"

"Like I said, environmental regulations. They almost made Earth unlivable a couple hundred years ago. Pigs are just too nasty to ranch more than a dozen or so in any one place there."

"Well, Earth was damned filthy, that's for sure. Almost as dirty as it was heavy. Anyway, pork's way too expensive for me. I wouldn't even be able to afford pork on Earth, let alone on Mars, so since I had a first class ticket and meals were covered, I wanted to try pork. So I told the servebot I wanted ham and beans.

"The stupid thing said there was no 'Hammond bean' listed in its database. So I said 'No, you stupid junk pile, ham, and, beans.' It said 'The word Hammond is not in my database.' stupid thing."

John grinned. "So what did you do?"

"What could I do? I ordered a barbecued pork steak. It was really good! But the damned robots annoyed me like that the whole trip. The very next morning I felt like a turkey cheese omelette so I ordered one. The stupid robot said 'There are no Turkish cheeses listed in the database.' So I said 'A turkey omelette with cheese.' So it says 'there are no Turkish omelette dishes listed in the database.' Stupid computer.

"So I said 'I want a cheese omelette with turkey meat. A turkey omelette has nothing to do with the country called Turkey...' What's so damned funny, John?"

John was laughing uproariously. "Exactly the same thing happened to Destiny when we first came here, only the computer was printing it out instead of talking. Let me guess, it said 'Parse error, please rephrase'."

"Yep, exactly. So I said I wanted an omelette with turkey meat, and it goes 'There is no meat that has come from that country listed in the database.' dumb machine! So I says 'Turkey the bird, damn it!' it said..."

"It said 'Parse error, please rephrase,' didn't it?" John interrupted.

"Sure did. So I asked what meats were available for omelettes. It said pork, chicken, duck, turkey, and beef. So I said 'A cheese omelette with turkey meat.' the idiotic thing repeated 'There is no meat from that country.' I'll tell you, John, that damned thing was really making me mad by then. I finally said 'Damn it, computer, I want a cheese omelette with bird meat.' it said 'Please name the bird.' I told it turkey and finally got my breakfast."

"There's a trick to it," John said. "Tell it you want a cheese and turkey omelette and it won't give you any trouble. If you would have asked for navy beans and ham you would have gotten your ham and beans. Like I said, they don't really think."

"No kidding. That must the dumbest computer I ever saw. Well, the tendbot in the commons may have been even more stupid. It didn't know what a Cardinal was."

John groaned. "Ed, that's strictly the Martian name for that drink. Everybody else calls them Bloody Marys."

"Oh. Why do they call them that?"

"Because that's what they were called for hundreds of years before anybody ever came here, before they had space travel, even. Before your ancestors ever left Earth."

"So why do we call them Cardinals then?"

"Frank Harris was responsible for the name. He was a farmer who came here from Earth and started growing tomatoes, under the 'Cardinal' brand."

"But why cardinal?"

"There's a bright red Earthian bird called a cardinal, so he named the bright red tomatoes after the bird. Bartenders here had never had a Bloody Mary before, because nobody here had tomatoes before Hardy brought them. So when they thought they had invented a tomato drink, they named it after the brand of tomatoes."

"How do you know all this stuff?"

"My wife's a history buff. She's been getting me interested in it, too. So what happened after you got to Earth?"

"Oh, man, it was pure hell, painful torture and terror. You know I've only been off Mars a few times in my life, mostly to Ceres or an asteroid dome out in the belt. But Earth... oh man. It was nothing like I'd ever experienced before. Or even imagined, it was horrible!

"First was the *weight!* That was part of what was wrong with the trip, when the robot was arguing about the turkey cheese omelette it was already getting really heavy. By the time we reached Earth I couldn't walk at all and had to use an electric chair to get around. How do those people live like that?"

"Ed, you should have been working out for months before going to Earth, especially since you've never had more than Mars gravity."

"Well, I did walk."

"Walking's not nearly enough."

"No kidding, I couldn't even stand up there. Had to have a robot help me in and out of bed. It was torture!"

"Why didn't you use a walker?"

"You have to have gravity close to Earth's to learn how to use one."

"Bill Holiday uses one, and he's from Ceres. All the asterites grew up in less gravity than you did and he goes to Earth all the time, it's part of his job."

"He would have had to train to use it, those things weigh over a hundred kilos counting the power, and training takes longer than I was going to be on Earth.

"The horrible weight was bad enough, but it was horribly scary there as well."

John grinned. He was an immigrant, who was born in St. Louis and had settled on Mars in late middle age. He hadn't thought of how it must be for a native-born Martian or Asterite on Earth. "Pretty scary, huh? I mean, not having a protective dome."

"Well, I've been outside the dome plenty of times, but being outside without an environment suit..." He shivered visibly. "Give me a shot of Scotch.

"It was night when we got there, and they used what seemed like they use here on Mars to connect the ship to the terminal. On Mars it's so passengers don't have to wear environment suits, but I don't know why they do it on Earth. Probably so us spacers would feel at home."

"Well, not really," John said. "It gets hot and cold there, and it rains. It's so passengers don't have to have coats and umbrellas. They were doing it like that before the first spacer dome was built."

"Yeah, I found out about rain and cold the night I got there, and heat the next day. In the entrance way to the terminal there was a flash in a window and a loud boom a second or two later. I thought there had been an explosion."

"Thunder."

"Yeah, and it was really loud! I almost jumped out of my skin. Anyway, we rented a car and I told it to take us to our hotel for check-in, and the first lightning flash scared the hell out of me. It looked like a crack in the sky and made me feel like all the air would escape, and then the thunder. I've never heard anything so loud!"

"You should hear a chemical rocket with a heavy load taking off!"

"I have, down here on Mars, and it's nowhere near as loud as thunder."

John laughed. "Ed, there's hardly any air outside the dome. Haven't you noticed how much quieter it is outside the dome?"

"There's nothing out there to make noise."

"Well, if there was it wouldn't be loud."

"I guess. Anyway, parking at the hotel was outside, but the car dropped us off under an awning before it parked itself. Lightning flashed again, and it really gave me the willies. Then it thundered, even louder than it had before. It was so loud you could *feel* the sound. It was really scary!" He finished his beer and slid his glass to the other side of the bar. "Fill 'er up, John!"

John poured another beer for Ed as Ed continued his traveling horror story. "Man, all that water pouring out of the sky. It was really strange, and even the water was scary and I don't know why. And it was *cold.* Must have been under twenty."

"It gets well below zero some places."

"How do they live like that?" he repeated. "I was all right as long as I was inside, except that first night when it stormed. I hated that storm! I sure am glad we don't have anything like that on Mars!

"There was a bar in the hotel, thankfully, so I didn't have to go out until the next morning. But the storm scared the hell out of me."

"So how did your meeting go?"

"Well, I had to take the car there, meaning I had to be outside. It was fine in the dark, like a room with no lights turned on, but walking outside without an environment suit when you could see the sky *really* freaked me out. I finally told myself it was just a big blue dome."

"Did it work?"

"Not really. It was really hard rolling around out there in my electric chair, and it was really hot outside! I never sweated before, and I hate it.

"But worse than that was bugs. Some of them bite. Some of the bugs they called 'butterflies' the Earthians thought were pretty. I thought they were creepy and scary.

"And barking dogs. I never saw a dog before, and John, those things are scary as hell, just downright terrifying. And there are a whole lot of them there."

"Okay, how did the meeting go?"

"Lousy. Between the weight and the storm I didn't sleep well. And the weight, the bugs, the dogs, the outside, the heat, the storm, all of it had me so rattled I couldn't think straight, and we didn't get the contract, DA2 did. At least it was a friend's dome.

"Give me another shot, John. Man, but I'm glad to be back home here on Mars. Earth sucks. Now I know what people mean by 'hell on Earth'. Earth *is* hell!"

John grinned again. “So... I take it you’re not going back?”

Professor Umlort was jumping for joy; he might even win the Xavel prize for his discovery! Fame and riches were to be his, he was sure. The funny thing was, he was looking for extragortofic life, but found an anomaly on the third planet of the Bingian system that was just downright inexplicably weird. The planet's giant satellite was rare enough, but this wasn't the first planet they'd found like that. The Zortarian system even had a double planet with both planets the exact same size, and what's more they were the same size as Gortof.

The professor nervously straightened his dorbray; he was to be interviewed on live telezonor in a few minutes about his discovery. "Borz", he said, "I sure am glad I majored in astronomy." A ziffle led him to the interview chamber.

"Live in three... two... one.." the director said, then pointed at the show's host.

"Good morning, Gortof! News is breaking this morning about a fantastic discovery in the Bingian system, and we have a live interview with Doctor Darly Umlort from the University of Lorp Central's astronomy department. Professor Umlort, early reports were that you had possibly discovered life on Bing 3, but you now say the planet is lifeless?"

"Yes sir, this is the strangest thing I've ever seen. It isn't life, but it behaves as if it were alive, like leaves in the wind do, only without the wind. There are structures on the planet that grow, from nothing, and they're composed of 100% inorganic material.

"But the strangest thing is the smaller, carbon based structures that seemingly move at random, with no rhyme or reason or apparent purpose. Don't get me wrong, these moving structures are gigantic. But these things aren't alive, either; at least, they're not life as we know it. Very interesting, indeed."

The interviewer grommed his rhytentles and said "Do you think your university will be sending a probe there?"

"No sir," Umlort replied. "It's ten thousand light years away. It would take our fastest probe five thousand years one way. That's a long time to wait for data."

"You say these objects move, I assume they aren't blown around by the wind or something?" asked the interviewer.

"We thought so at first, but further study showed that what's going on there should be impossible according to everything we know. These objects seem to be alive, but they can't possibly be. First, they're mostly made of dihydrogen monoxide and various forms of carbon and other materials. Science fiction writers have gone on and on about 'carbon based life forms', and although it could theoretically be possible, in practicality the only life we've found has been based on similar chemistry to our own. Besides, the atmosphere of this planet is mostly inert nitrogen, with a lot of pure, poisonous, oxygen. If they were alive, how would they breathe? And with so much dihydrogen monoxide on the planet—it's mostly covered in the vile substance—it actually rains down from the atmosphere!"

He continued, "What's strangest about this planet is the weak electromagnetic radiation that comes from it. The radiation is the strangest of all; this planet seems to be a giant magnet!"

"Wow," said the interviewer, "Imagine what life would be like here if Gortof were a giant magnet!"

The doctor chuckled. “It would be lifeless. The magnetism would keep the star’s most important radiations, such as gamma rays, away from it.”

The interviewer would have shuddered had he been human, but since he was Gortofian he swanndiged (which is nothing like shuddering). “My Grodling! You would starve in a planet like that!”

“Indeed,” replied the doctor. “Life couldn’t even begin to start on a place like that, which makes the objects we’ve seen so strange. Our chemists and physicists can’t explain how things work there.”

“So, what’s next, Doctor?”

“More study, of course. The next generation of telescopes will measure frequencies of light almost all the way down to ultraviolet, far lower than the frequencies of light we can discern without the aid of mechanical apparatus. And it will be able to resolve all the way down to a single micrometer, even from here. Of course, with the lower frequencies you don’t get such a good resolution, but the data are fascinating."

“Will you still be on the forefront of the search for extragortofian life, Professor?”

“Well, of course, but we’re going to be studying this strange place a lot. There may even be a brand new science that evolves from this study.”

“Thank you, doctor, that was very interesting.”

“You’re very welcome. And thank you, sir.”

“Next up,” said the interviewer, “a look at the new forgantribles, just in time for flogardsmalia! And now a word from our sponsor...”

"Mark! I haven't seen you in two years!"

"Haven't been to Mars. Been carrying ores from the belt to Earth. I heard you got married?"

"Yeah, Destiny's the best thing that happened to me. Met her on the trip here, she's an astronomer. She's building a new kind of telescope right outside the dome. What are you drinking, Mark?"

"Beer, I guess. Been a long damned time since I had a beer."

John was already filling a mug from a tapper. "Have one on me. I'm making my own now even though I sell import. Best beer on Mars, I think. I'm pretty proud of it."

"Where's all your customers?"

"Where are my customers?? Hell, Mark, it's nine in the morning! The hard core alcoholics don't start showing up until ten."

He handed the mug to Mark, who took a sip. "Damn, John, you're right, this is some damned good beer! Hell, your lager is better than Guinness!"

"Well, thanks. I have pilsner, ale, and wheat beer, too. Took some chemistry and beer making classes, and brewed a lot of real crap before I got any good at it. Since I brew it here it's the cheapest beer on the planet."

Mark looked at his mug and laughed. "Can't get much cheaper than free."

"That's a two dollar beer you're drinking. Guinness is ten bucks, fifteen for a can."

"No bottles?"

"You won't find much bottled beer on Mars, and if you do it will be expensive as hell. Bottles break too easy; I'm sure glad the beer I brought when we came here was in cans, I'd have had a hell of a mess on my houseboat!"

"Why?"

"Pirates were after us, more than even exist now, I hear. The maneuvers I had to do to stay alive would have popped every damned beer in the boat open if it had been in bottles. How is the pirate situation these days?"

"I haven't had pirates mess with me in a couple of years. They're sure to try to regroup, though, but Ramos' fleet is doing a damned good job."

"Yeah, Dewey told me last week that even though the fleet was to cut losses, we're making money on it. Every boat Ramos captures from the pirates is a huge recovery fee from whatever company owns the boat, and the other companies are paying us to guard them now. Ready for another?"

Mark looked at his mug. "Yeah, fill 'er up. Damn but you make good beer! Tell me, what's that huge poster on the wall about? A guy with a peg leg and a guitar wearing a funny costume, an eye patch, and a green bird on his shoulder?"

John grinned. "That's John Lee Hoo... uh, oh, watch your language, Mark, she's mean.

"Good Morning, Mrs. Ferguson! The usual?" he asked, reaching for a gin bottle.

"No, my pension check doesn't come in for another week and I'm almost broke; that damned Earthian gin costs way too God damned much and I can't afford another martini. I'll have one of your pilsners instead."

John poured a glass and handed it to her and turned back to Mark. "Like I was saying, that's John Lee Hooker. Hear that music? That's him."

The jukebox was singing "You's a dirty mother, babe! Ain't no... no ugly good..."

"He was an old blues singer from the twentieth century, one of the greats of classical guitar."

"He had one eye and a peg leg? And what's with the bird?"

A sloppily dressed man in need of a shave came in, his hands shaking badly. John poured him a beer and grinned. "No, that was put in by an image manipulation program, he had two good eyes and two good legs. He's dressed as an eighteenth century pirate."

"But why?"

"The trip here. I had two hundred drug addicted hookers on board and we were attacked by more pirates than anyone had seen before; the hookers saved us. A thought hit me on the trip that I was Captain Hooker with two hundred peter panhandlers."

The old lady laughed. "Nice story, John, but it's bullshit. You aren't old enough to have been a shipping captain." John and Mark looked at each other and laughed.

"What's so funny?" the woman asked, with a glare.

"Private joke," John said. "Only funny to us. Nothing to do with you."

She said "This beer isn't doing it, you have anything stronger that doesn't cost an arm and a leg?"

"Well, yes, but you might not like it. This is *really* strong stuff; white lightning. When a batch of beer turns out to not be very good I distill it down to nearly pure ethanol. Want me to make you a martini out of it?"

"What's it cost?"

"Buck a shot."

"Sure."

The shaking man said "I'll have one, too. Make it a double. Not a martini, just two shots."

John poured "Mister Shaky" a drink and mixed Mrs. Ferguson's martini, and handed it to her as the man downed his shot. He stopped shaking. Mrs. Ferguson sipped her martini.

"Whoo-EEE! Whoo! Wow, John, now *that's* a martini!" She shivered and grinned, and took another sip.

"While you're pouring, I'm empty," Mark said. John poured him a beer, and a beer and a shot for the formerly shaky gentleman.

"Be careful," John said, "You've been traveling. How long since you had a beer?"

"I had one on the station on Titan maybe six months ago."

John laughed. "Ship time or planet time?"

"How the hell should I know? Anyway, what difference does it make?"

"It depends. Can you afford to get drunk today?"

"No, I plan on passing out by noon. That last trip was hell."

"Why? What happened?"

Mrs. Ferguson and the other man were drinking silently. Mark said "That asshole drunk fuckhead Jones."

"Larry Jones?"

"Of course, Bob Jones and Roy Jones are good guys. Larry's a stupid asshole. Could have got me killed. I think he tried to kill me."

Mrs. Ferguson started giggling and asked for another martini. John poured it while Mark continued.

"He was drunk, of course, and piloting a ship that was on its way in to Titan when I was on my way out. Damned drunken idiot thought I was a pirate; at least, that's what he said, anyway. Bastard launched an atomic at me."

"Did it do any damage?"

"Hell yes, it was only a hundred meters away from my boat when it went off. There was only a little physical damage to the starboard dock, but the EMP killed a generator and six engines. They ought to put spare circuit boards for those things in storage, I came to Mars on one generator.

"The blast moved the whole damned ship and threw me across the room. Broke my left arm in three places and four ribs on my left side. God damn but it hurt! If I ever see that asshole Jones again I'm going to..."

Mrs. Ferguson started laughing riotously, slipped off her stool and started to stagger out. "Those two young boys piloting space ships for decades!" she said, and started laughing again as she went through the door.

The thirsty fellow asked for another beer and said "I don't know, guys, you do look awful young."

"I'll explain it in a minute," John said. "So the asshole broke your arm and ribs?"

"Yeah, the stupid son of a bitch. He should know there's no pirates there. I think he was lying. I won a shitload of money playing poker with the stupid drunk six months earlier and I think he was trying to kill me. I was hoping he'd get prosecuted, but they just fired the lucky bastard.

"Now, Mister... what did you say your name was?" he said, turning to the stranger, who grinned.

"I didn't. Rob Black. You're...?"

"Mark Wilson. I saw the playbills, are you the guitar player from Earth?"

"Yeah, that's me. So the bartender here said he'd explain..."

"John Knolls," John said. "Look, Mister Black, they knew about relativity hundreds of years ago."

"They may have, I don't."

"Okay, it's easy. The faster you go, the slower time goes."

"Why?"

"Hell if I know, my wife might. But that's how it works."

"It don't make no sense to me."

"Well look, suppose you could go at the speed of light..."

"That's stupid."

"Yes, of course you can't but suppose you could. If you could jump up instantly at the speed of light towards a planet around Alpha Proxima..."

"It has planets?"

"I don't know, you'd have to ask my wife. Suppose it does and you could jump there at the speed of light. Well, it would seem to you that the trip took less than a blink of an eye, but to people on Mars it would take four years."

"You guys are a riot!" He said laughing, left a ten dollar tip on the bar and left, still laughing.

"Dumb tourist!" Mark said. "Fill me up!"

The Accidental Traveler

The breakthrough was not in physics itself, but in mathematics. The new insights led physicists to see physics in a new light, and it wasn't long before they were experimenting with the equations, which seemed to indicate that it might be possible to instantly transport an object to anywhere in the universe.

It was a quarter century before a machine using the new understandings that actually did anything at all had any result, and the result was completely unexpected.

The apparatus was set up and turned on. A mouse seemed to come from nowhere, scurrying across the room as mice do. One of the participants shrieked, startled, but no one saw a connection between their experiment, which had seemingly failed yet again, and the unexpected intruder.

"Lets try it again," a grad student suggested. Doctor Phillips laughed, and said "Doing the same thing the same way and expecting it to work is insane."

"I'm not suggesting we do it exactly the same way. Let's try a higher voltage."

"Well, voltage is one part of the equation that's a little fuzzy. Same wattage, or raise voltage and leave amperage alone?"

"We could try both."

"Go ahead, but I'm not expecting any different results."

The student set the experiment back up, doubled the input voltage, and turned the device on. A large wild boar appeared in the room close to the wall. They all ran in fright, closed the door, and called animal control. Animal control caught the hog, which was taken to the municipal zoo.

Gabriel Watkins had a different job to do today than yesterday; his mule would get a break from the plowing. There was a wild boar that was upsetting his animals and would be trampling his fields and eating his produce if he didn't do anything. He had a pig to hunt, kill, butcher, and eat.

It was otherwise a normal morning like any other. He read *The Spectator* and drank coffee as his wife prepared breakfast. The newspaper was talking about the new president, James Monroe. It also spoke of the nation's newest state, Maine. Everyone had expected that for weeks, since the Missouri Compromise had been signed. Missouri was sure to become a state soon.

After he finished his breakfast he loaded all three of his muskets and both of his pistols, told his wife he would be back before lunch and set off towards the woods.

The boar wasn't hard to find. He raised his musket, aimed—and the animal disappeared before his eyes. He scratched his head, and the woods themselves disappeared, replaced with mowed grass and brick buildings.

Officer Oscar Jobs of the SIU campus police department was shocked. A heavily armed man was on the campus! He drew his weapon and ordered the man to drop his weapons and get on the ground. This was especially disturbing, since all of law enforcement was on high alert because the Twin Towers and part of the Pentagon had been destroyed that morning.

Oscar was greatly relieved when the suspect complied.

Because of the terrorism, the news of the armed man on campus didn't even hit the *Edwardsville Intelligencer,* let alone the *St. Louis Post-Dispatch.*

"This is the strangest case I've ever seen," Dr. Wilson said to Dr. Kent. "The man is obviously suffering from schizophrenia, and the type of schizophrenia isn't that uncommon. What's weird is that his whole persona, and not just the fantasy in his mind, all corroborate. He swears that he was born in 1790, that he's a thirty one year old farmer and it's spring of 1821. He was wearing antique clothing from the era and carrying antique firearms; front loading muskets. All of the antiques were in excellent shape for their age, almost two hundred years old. He claims to have owned the muzzle loading weapons for a decade.

"Really strange. Anyway, Haldol isn't having any effect except to put him to sleep. I've hit a brick wall. Any suggestions?"

They didn't repeat the experiment for another year to allow the theorists to scratch their heads and do calculations. It was, as it often is, one of the graduate students who was close to writing his doctoral thesis who found the answer, or what appeared to be the answer. Rather than sending objects away from the device, it brought them closer to it. They changed some circuitry and repeated it.

It failed spectacularly.

"Dr. Wilson, your patient has escaped."

"What? When? How?"

"We just discovered him missing and we're faced with a mystery. Everything was properly secured, none of the guards saw anything, the cameras trained on the doors saw nothing. He just disappeared into thin air."

"That poor man! I hope he's okay until he gets picked up again."

"There's more, it gets even weirder. His clothing was laying on the bed, laid out like someone laying there but he hadn't stuffed them with anything, and I just got a call that all of his antiques are missing, and nothing else from storage was gone. No sign of forced entry, the door was locked when they went to do inventory."

It was two o'clock, and Emma was worried. Her husband was still gone, and fearing for him went in search. She was afraid that the boar, or perhaps some other animal, might have gotten the best of him.

She found him at the edge of the woods, naked and sleeping, with his clothing and other belongings scattered around him. She almost didn't recognize him; his beard was gone and his hair was clipped short, but she saw the scar on his leg. He had thought he would lose that leg, but God had been good to them.

She touched his cheek and he woke up.

"Emma? Where am I? Where are my clothes? What am I doing here? Dear Jesus, I had the strangest dream!"

"Are you all right, Gabe?"

"I don't know. The strangest thing... where is my clothing?"

"Scattered all around you. What happened to your beard and hair?"

He touched his face. "Dear sweet Jesus, Emma, it had to be that damned witch!"

"Alice?"

"Who else? You know that old crone hates me and it's the only explanation. Emma, she somehow transported me to some sort of magical but evil place. I don't know how I got back. I was in some sort of prison and went to sleep, and when you woke me up I was here, not far from where I was when... Oh, good Lord, this is terrible!" He started getting dressed and gathering his belongings. "We need to see the sheriff. That witch needs to hang!"

"What did you see?"

"Well, I had the hog in my sights and he flat out just disappeared without a trace. Then everything else was gone and I was somewhere else and a man with what looked like a weapon of some sort, although it wasn't like any gun I ever saw ordered me to drop my guns and get on the ground, and I did.

"He tied my hands behind my back with some sort of metal thing and put me in a really strange thing, made of what looked like painted metal but really shiny, on four black wheels that didn't look anything like any wheel I've ever seen. The thing had seats. He got in it in front of me, did some things, and *it started moving!* All by itself! And *really* fast, faster than I've seen anything go.

"And then he talked into a small black thing and it answered!

"They put ink on my fingers, rubbed them on paper, and flashed something in my face. Then they put me in a tiny stone room with a steel door.

"Then they took me, with their witchy magic things, to another place, some sort of jail where they pretended to be nice. There was lots more magic, a crystal ball that showed moving pictures and had sound, it was really weird.

"Then they filled me with magic potions that dulled my mind and made me sleep. Someone they called a doctor, some woman, kept asking me stupid questions almost every day.

"Then one night I went to sleep and you woke me up here. We need to talk to the preacher and the sheriff, that witch needs to die!

It took another century for the theorists to figure it out. The mistake they had made was not realizing that time and space are inseparable; that there is no difference, that time is just another dimension.

The sheriff said there was nothing he could legally do, but Alice Chalmers was hung by a lynch mob on May 12, 1821. No one was charged with or prosecuted for her murder.

Trouble on Ceres

"Bill! Where've you been? I thought you said you were going to spend your vacation here on Mars?"

"Up on Ceres for the last three weeks, give me a beer. Make it one of your lagers. They had a real bad emergency up there, and my boat was the only one close enough and fast enough to do any good. They were to do maintenance while I was vacationing, but postponed it for Ceres. Orion Transport had a ship here on Mars, too, but you know better than anybody that their ships are only a third or less as fast as ours. Hell, you used to be a captain and you're on the Green-Osbourne board of directors.

"Everyone would have been dead when the Orion boat got there if we didn't have one of our ships here. They sent it anyway, with even more batteries. They would have needed 'em."

John, the bartender and owner, replied "Yeah, I talked to Chuck. He called as soon as it happened. I didn't know you ran the rescue boat. Sorry about your vacation."

"Well, it was just postponed and I'm on vacation now. So Chuck called?"

Chuck Watson, mayor of the habitat dome on Ceres, was shaking as he put down the phone. It was one of the worst catastrophes possible on an asteroid dome; or in his case, a dwarf planet dome. It would have been even worse up on Mars, with the gigantic domes that had been built on that planet, with all of the people living in them. Of course, on Mars they would have all the supplies they would need, considering how many domes were up there.

But still, there were twenty thousand people down here on Ceres, the mining robot operators and the tradespeople and service people and repair people necessary for normal life, and all of their children. And they had less than twenty minutes to get inside a building, as the dome was leaking air, and leaking badly. The sirens went off in everyone's pockets and purses immediately after the power went out and the battery-powered emergency lighting lit up.

Buildings inside domes were designed for this sort of emergency. They were airtight when the windows were closed, which was seldom; temperatures in the domes were comfortable whether one was inside or outside a building. But when alarms went off, windows closed by themselves. The doors to the outside of buildings opened inwards, and most buildings even had airlocks. Commercial buildings had at least one person-sized airlock at their entrances and exits, and a home's garage served as the house's airlock. Anyone not home who didn't have a garage would have to find shelter elsewhere, because there was no getting inside or outside a building without an airlock when the dome's pressure dropped too low.

Chuck called his old friend Charlie Onehorse, mayor of Dome Australia Two on Mars, hoping there was a Green-Osbourne ship there, and hoping there were enough supplies on Mars. Nobody but G-O had ships that were fast enough to get here in time, and he wasn't sure they would survive even if one of that company's ships were on Mars. The message would be a while getting to Mars, even though luckily the two bodies' orbits were relatively close right now.

"You're a dumb arse," the London-born Chuck told himself when he got off the phone, and called another friend living in a different Martian dome, John Knolls. John owned his favorite Martian bar and quite a bit of Green-Osbourne stock, was on G-O's board of directors, and his wife was the daughter of one of that company's founders. If there was a ship available, John could get it here. If he didn't, more people would die. In fact, he was afraid that everybody might die.

Two were killed in the blast, and three were already dying from radiation sickness. Several more people were injured, four of them critically. There had been an accident in the fusion-powered electrical generators; one of the chambers that the fusion took place in exploded. The entire place was now toxic, and many of the survivors probably wouldn't survive in the long run.

It wasn't, of course, a fusion explosion. A fusion explosion would have leveled the dome and instantly incinerated everyone there. It was a chemical explosion, and it would likely take months to find the accident's initial cause.

Buildings in domes were always built with a dome leak in mind, and that was the problem in this case. The reactor was built against and as part of a dome wall. It was built intentionally thin behind the generating plant, far less sturdy than the rest of the building's walls, so if the unlikely chamber explosion ever actually happened, the force and radiation would go outside the dome.

It worked perfectly, except that some of the building's seams weren't quite strong enough. Luckily the whole building didn't give way or everyone outside at the time would have died instantly. But there were cracks around the doors and air was leaking badly.

It was a matter of time now. Air inside buildings would only last so long, and many had no extra oxygen.

"Holy crap," John said when he read Chuck's phone call from Ceres. He called the main office on Mars, which was in his dome, and ordered that a ship be readied immediately.

"We only have two here, sir. One is due for maintenance, and the other one is stranded in orbit with two badly damaged generators waiting for a shipment of parts from Earth."

"Reschedule the maintenance on the one that flies and get it and its pilot ready, and I mean now. This is a real emergency."

He then called his friend Ed Waldo, who was mayor of his dome. He'd need Ed's help coordinating everything. Maybe Ed would come by his bar later on when he got off from work.

Karen Wilkerson was chief engineer at the power station on Ceres, and was watching the board closely before it happened. One of the techs had pointed out some abnormal readings, and when she saw the blue line spike she hit the evacuation alarm immediately, saving a lot of lives. Had she not seen it coming, everyone in the building would have died. Instead, the only casualties were those who didn't drop everything and leave the building immediately, and one who had fallen down in her rush to escape and had broken her arm.

Now she was in the annex, worrying about her people. She had already called Dome Hall with the disaster alert. Now all there was to do was to wait until the leaks were patched and a supply ship came with batteries, because they wouldn't be generating any electricity from this generator again and building a new one would take months.

And wait for air, of course. If that ship didn't get here on time everyone would likely die.

Commander Jose Ramos and the Green-Osbourne Security fleet that he was in charge of were in orbit around Mars, as usual, when he saw the pirates. "*¡Santo mierde!*" he swore in his native Spanish. That was an awful lot of pirates, more than he'd seen together for years. He set course towards them, and when the pirates saw Ramos' fleet they took off. The G-O Security ships took chase.

A call came in from G-O headquarters. Transport 487-B was missing, and they believed that it was now in the hands of pirates. It had been stranded in orbit around Mars, waiting for parts for generator repairs. When the first transport showed up with its parts, the ship was gone. The repair facility's crew was missing, hadn't even radioed, and was presumed dead.

He swore again. Where was that damned Jones? Jones' ship was supposed to be guarding the orbiting repair facility that held 487-B. He worried about Bob and his crew, praying that they had simply been disabled by a mechanical malfunction before getting there. He cursed himself; he shouldn't have let Larry leave until Bob got there.

He then cursed himself for stupidity again; there was no way any pirate could beat Bob and his ship and crew. It must have been a mechanical malfunction.

He wondered how many of the facilities' personnel had been killed. Damn. There were three orbiting facilities, each with a G-O security ship guarding it, except the ship guarding this one was missing. And it was his responsibility; he should never have let Larry leave no matter how long he had been since he'd eaten or slept. This, he swore, would never happen again.

This was bad. Ever since the piracy had started not long after Mars was colonized, all space vessels were armed to some degree, but G-O ships were the best built, most heavily armored and heavily armed. Transport ships owned by Green-Osborne even had EMPs, atomics, and rail guns, and the security fleet was armed and armored even better. An atomic explosion wouldn't even damage a G-O craft, whether transport or security, unless it detonated closer than two hundred meters away. They were completely impervious to EMP blasts, which took out any electronics on anyone else's ships.

Now that pirates had a G-O ship...

Bill Kelly was sound asleep when the alarm went off on his phone. It was his boss, who told him he had a half an hour to be in the pilot seat ready for takeoff.

He rolled out of bed and swore. Not having time for a shower or breakfast, he hurriedly dressed and rushed to the spaceport.

"Glad you got here so fast, Bill," his boss told him. "There's a terrible disaster up on Ceres. Their power generator blew up and caused a huge air leak. We would have called sooner but I knew you'd be sleeping. You need to get those batteries and tanks of solid oxygen and nitrogen to the belt as fast as you can make that ship go. The robots should be done loading in ten or fifteen minutes."

Bill flew his houseboat to the ship and entered, belted into the pilot seat, and detached from the repair facility. Now he only had to wait for the countdown to leave orbit to begin as the ship drifted slowly away from the repair station.

The captain of the ship guarding the facility came on the radio. "You're on your own for a while, buddy. Commander Ramos says I need to join the chase against an awful lot of pirates, so keep your eyes open."

"I take off in five minutes anyway," Bill said. "I'll be okay."

"Well, I'll check on you shortly."

The pirates split up and ran in different directions. The Green-Osbourne defense fleet split up to chase them, and Commander Ramos went after the biggest one. It might be the stolen transport.

"*¿Qué en el infierno?*" It was outrunning him! That shouldn't be possible. Maybe it was an old fission ship that had been converted to fusions. When converting them from fission generators to fusions, the engineers had left the fission generator as a backup to the fusions, which often malfunctioned back then. Apparently the pirates had done a bit of hardware hacking and had made it so that they were using all three generators at once. He shook his head, when the company got that one back it was going to really need a lot of work. They might even have to scrap it.

Not only were Green-Osbourne ships heavily armed and armored, they were also stealthy. But not invisible, not as long as the engines were running, since they left a trail of ions behind. Jose grinned at this; common knowledge was that they were completely invisible. Common knowledge is often incorrect, although they were indeed invisible unless you knew what to look for.

It looked like the pirate was circling back towards Mars. He kept following the trail.

Will Welton was relieved. His crew had finally finished sealing off the generator building, putting plates and glue on the doorways and sealing the smaller leaks by the dome wall. But the danger was far from over, as the dome itself had practically no air pressure at all now. Rather than going back to the shop, he went home, thankful that his house had a garage that doubled as an airlock. If it didn't he would have had to stay in the shop until air arrived. All he could do now was wait for the supply ship to come, and hope his air held out long enough. "I need to get some house plants," he told himself.

When he got home he took off his helmet and gloves, and shut off the environment suit's power and valves, but didn't remove the suit; he didn't know how long his house's air would last. There was two hours worth of air left in its tank, and if his house ran out of air he'd need it. He wondered if anyone would live.

Bill was barely out of orbit before pirates were after him, and a lot of them, too. And wouldn't you know it, none of the Green-Osbourne defense fleet was anywhere near Mars where they usually were. Probably still chasing the other pirates, he thought, and here there were more. Well, Ralph had warned him, but he wished Jeff could have stuck around.

There was a lot more piracy now, ever since the trouble on Earth had started. The company's defense fleet was busier than it had ever been.

Pirates could be pretty clever at times, and may have lured the defense fleet away somehow. They had once infiltrated company maintenance years ago and sabotaged Bill's ship when it was being worked on. If it hadn't had been for John, who was a company captain at the time, he'd have been dead.

"God damn it," he swore out loud. "Not now! Pirates are the last thing I need. People are going to die if I don't get to Ceres!"

But pirates don't mind people dying. In fact, they quite often caused it. They seemed to enjoy killing.

He could have simply outrun them, but instead dropped an EMP set to discharge when it was right in the middle of the fleet that was after his boat. That should end the problem, and since it would kill everything electronic, the ships' life control systems would also be dead. If the salvage fleet didn't show up in time the pirates would be, too.

He hoped so. An awful lot of his friends had been killed at the hands of pirates. The only good pirate was a dead pirate, but he was okay with bad pirates rotting in prison.

His EMP didn't disable them all. Bad aim on his part? Half a dozen were still accelerating.

He dropped an atomic. He hated destroying valuable space ships that would get a bonus for him if there was a finder's fee involved, but it seemed the right thing to do at the time.

The lead ship survived. "Damn, they have one of ours," he said aloud, wondering how pirates had gotten hold of a virtually invincible G-O ship. He quickly called headquarters informing them that pirates had a company transport, although they were certainly aware of it, he thought. This was real trouble. G-O ships were faster, better armed, and sturdier (and usually larger) than other companies' ships. Now the pirates had EMPs and atomics!

But Bill knew these ships, and knew them better than most company captains, let alone any pirate. Bill was a nerd who loved not only studying how they worked, but how to make them work better. He'd gotten a third gravity on batteries once, and nobody else had ever managed to. Even though he'd tried to explain to the company engineers how he did it, they still didn't understand.

He'd outrun that sucker.

It took hours, but he did. He was running on both generators and batteries, which he'd set up when he realized that the pirates had one of his company's boats. He wondered why he wasn't pulling ahead of the pirate any faster than he was, especially since it was an old ship after him that he should have been able to outrun easily, even without the extra boost from the batteries. He hoped the extra wattage didn't harm any of the engines; this was a bit of his own nerdy design, the craft already was overdue for maintenance, and he had to run like this far longer than he thought he'd have to.

When he was far enough ahead of the pirate ship that he could no longer detect it, he went at full thrust for another two hours. Then he disconnected the batteries from the engines and set them charging from the generators as he continued on at the ship's normal top speed. His boss had told him to go as fast as he could make it go, but he worried about the maintenance issues.

He still hadn't had a shower or breakfast. He remedied that immediately.

Mayor Watson paced in his office, cursing himself. Why weren't there more oxygen generators? They had existed since the late twentieth century when they were used to treat emphysema, long before that disease was cured. There were a few in Dome Ceres, of course, but not many. Not nearly enough for an emergency like this.

There weren't many plants inside buildings, either, except inside the farm buildings. There were a lot of plants outside, but outdoor plants would do little good now; they'd die quickly without air, and in the cold. They would be a help in a home or business, changing the carbon dioxide people exhaled into oxygen and plant material, and he vowed to get plants in every building. Lots of them. Plants inside buildings would save lives!

And why didn't he have enough air for this sort of emergency stored away? He swore that there would be enough if something like this ever happened again. He cursed himself again for his lack of foresight.

Well, hindsight would have to do. If He lived. He'd gotten a message from John that a ship full of air and batteries was on its way, but would it get here on time?

The company defense fleet's commander never lost the ion trail, and eventually came up on the pirate ship, which was drifting through space at a high rate of speed. Either its engines had all burned out, or more likely all three of its generators had malfunctioned; it had been waiting for parts, and the pirates had probably installed old used, sub-par equipment. The other pirate vessels had been traveling along side, apparently trying to get the disabled craft going again. They took off in different directions, maybe five of them; his fleet had taken the rest when he was chasing the pirate Green-Osbourne transport.

He got a message from Bob Jones that he and his crew were safe. It had indeed been a mechanical problem, and he was at one of the repair facilities in orbit around Mars, cursing about the stolen transport. If only... And Ramos was still cursing himself for letting Larry leave before his replacement showed up. He wasn't going to do that again!

Docking with the crippled purloined transport was easy, and now his commandos were all on duty. He wondered how many pirates would be captured, and how many killed. He gave no thought to G-O casualties, because there never were any. These men and women were very well trained.

He chuckled. When pirates fought with the police on Earth, often the pirates won. But never when they tangled with the G-O security fleet. Earth had better never go to war with Mars!

Bill fretted. Engine 129 was showing a small undervoltage in one computer, and a small overvoltage on a different computer. All four computers were supposed to agree. He trudged down the five flights of stairs, worrying and cursing. He was half a day from Ceres, his time, but it would be longer Ceres time because of the time dilation that extreme speed causes. If he lost any more engines... and God forbid that he lose a generator. Everyone on Ceres would die, including Chuck.

Even though two of the four computers disagreeing usually meant a bad electrical connection, he shut number 129 down, as per normal operation. He considered shutting the two next to it down as well, knowing that sometimes this sort of problem spread from engine to engine. One engine wouldn't matter, since he was ahead of schedule, sort of, but three might.

He'd probably broken another speed record and would arrive "early", if there was such a thing in a situation like this. He'd been doing more than a gravity and a half when the pirate ship was chasing him, which was as high as the indicator would go. The craft's top speed was supposed to be one point four Gs, and he wondered how much he'd really gotten out of it. Walking up those five flights of stairs in that gravity was a real workout, especially after being on Mars and on low gravity runs.

Unlike most runs, he spent most of his waking time the whole run in the pilot room, the engine room at the bottom of the ship, and traveling between the two. "My legs will look like turkey legs when this run's over," he panted as he climbed the stairs.

It was time to turn the ship around and decelerate, and he was glad it wasn't an old boat. The old models almost always had something break when you reversed them for braking. If he lost a generator now, he'd overshoot Ceres.

On Ceres it had been two Earthian days since the accident, and things were getting grim. Some people were running out of food, air was getting pretty bad in some buildings, and if the ship ran late a lot of people would die. Maybe everyone.

Will Welton had taken off the suit finally, realizing he couldn't keep wearing it until air came. He'd put it back on if the air in his house got thick.

Mayor Watson had spent that time mostly pacing in his office, feeling like a caged animal. Most Cererians were probably feeling the same way, he thought.

While he paced, the same thoughts raced through his head, over and over, planning for the aftermath of this mess. Dome Ceres was going to have emergency oxygen, and a lot more inside plants. He envisioned air pipes running into homes from a central emergency air supply that would run parallel to water pipes. He wondered why this hadn't been done before, and wondered what else he could do to make the Cererian Dome safer. All he could do now was hope that ship wasn't late.

Jen Carpenter was in the hospital with a broken arm. She had panicked when she had a strange feeling and started running, and was outside before the alarms even sounded. She didn't even know what had spooked her. The first one out of the building, she tripped and fell right when the alarm sounded.

Her arm hurt, but she was glad of her misstep, because hospitals keep lots of oxygen. The folks there would be the last to asphyxiate if that ship was late.

A tear ran down her cheek; she had lost friends in the accident, and probably wouldn't even get to attend the funerals.

Chuck answered his phone. It was his Martian friend Captain Bill Kelly, piloting the rescue ship. He was only a half hour away, planet time! He hadn't expected it to arrive until the next Earth day. Nobody counted Cererian days, since they were so short.

"Thank God!" he said over the phone to Captain Kelly.

Bill laughed in the weirdly fast, high pitch of someone on an approaching ship coming in at high speeds. "Thank pirates. They have one of our ships and I had to do what might have been dangerous to outrun 'em. I'm pretty sure I broke a speed record. Look, Chuck, suit up and I'll meet you at the transport dock. Ceres' gravity is low enough I can land an ion ship on the surface."

They spoke for another minute or two before hanging up. Bill readied the ship for landing, and Chuck suited up to meet him.

Will Welton was worried. Oxygen was getting low and carbon dioxide was getting thick in his house, and he was afraid he'd better drive to the hospital before he started suffering from anoxia. He donned his environment suit, helmet, and gloves, turned on the valves and electronics, and went into his garage/airlock to drive to the hospital. Surely they would have enough oxygen.

He got in the car, pumped the air back into the house from the garage, opened the garage door, started it up—and it wouldn't lift.

Even though Ceres is classified as a dwarf planet, it still doesn't have much gravity, so wheeled vehicles simply wouldn't have enough traction to be very useful. So vehicles were hovercraft, with fans lifting and propelling the vehicle like an early twenty first century multi-fan drone.

But fans don't work when there's no air to fan. He got out and started walking to the hospital.

His CO_2 alarm went off. He kept walking.

His low oxygen alarm went off. He kept walking.

Confused by the anoxia he was starting to suffer, he had a hard time finding the hospital. His head was pounding, and his mood was swinging like a yo-yo. He finally reached the hospital two hours later and collapsed in the emergency room's airlock.

It was only a minute or two before he was found, as he wasn't the only one who had started running out of air. Hospital staff were extra busy today!

"I sure am glad to see you, mate. Things are getting desperate," said the British Chuck.

"I hope I got here on time," Bill replied.

"Barely, but yeah. Once those canisters are finished unloading and opened they'll melt and boil away quickly in this warmth." The robots were bringing them in and opening them, and the first ones opened were already appreciably less full. Clouds of vapor were rolling out of the boiling but super-cold liquid in the opened canisters.

Bill looked at the thermometer on his environment suit's sleeve. Warmth? Oh, well. "So how long will it be until you can get a new generator built?"

"Six months. It would only take two if we could afford speed, but we're going to need so many batteries our budget is going to be really strained."

"Why don't you call John and see if the company will rent this ship to you for a couple of months?"

"I don't need a ship, I need electricity!"

"What do you think this tub runs on, hydrazine? There are two fusion generators on it, big ones, three stories tall each. We dock ships that have busted generators and charge the broken ship's backup batteries all the time.

"My boat was going to be out of action for a while anyway for maintenance, and considering what I did to get here alive and on time it's really going to need it. Maintenance should be easier with gravity, even as low a gravity as Ceres has. We could send the dozen or so people necessary to do it here. Call John. I'll bet he'd do it for a load of rare earths, and you folks have plenty!"

"Come on, Bill, lets get to my office so I can call him, that's a great idea!"

"Look, Chuck, I'd love to, but I need to supervise hooking the ship's generators up to your grid so everybody can charge their batteries. I'll meet you at the Bull's Head for a beer later if it's open."

"It should be. Every restaurant, pub, and shop on the dome will be busy tonight. Cooped up in their homes running out of air they're going to want to be out, and only a fool would leave his shop closed. I'll meet you there."

"Yeah, Chuck called, twice."

"I thought his staff would have."

"I don't know, I couldn't exactly talk to him there. It was email, of course, but I can't see Chuck not handling something like that himself. So how was your trip? What happened after you got to Ceres?"

"Well, there was nothing out of the ordinary on the way there, just routine. You were a captain once, you know how it goes." He chuckled. "I'm pretty sure I broke a speed record, though."

John laughed. "It wouldn't be the first time."

"Well, anyway, a couple of hours after I got there you could walk around outside without an environment suit, and half the people there opened their windows because the cold, thin air outside was more breathable than the thick, oxygen-thin and carbon dioxide-saturated air inside.

"The police checked all of the buildings to make sure the occupants were all right, and I met Chuck at the pub when we were done working.

"I was on Ceres for a long time, rode back on the Orion ship after it finally got there, unloaded all the batteries, and loaded a shipment of rare earths for Charlie Onehorse's dome here on Mars. As slow as Orion's ships are I was on Ceres a week before he even got there, and it took half a day to unload the batteries and load the ore.

"So how have things been down here on Mars?"

This has been an exciting time for us, and not just the scientists, everyone on board is really excited. Even me, and you know me, nothing gets me excited. We found another stellar system harboring life in this galaxy, and this one is really, really weird. It's unbelievably, unimaginably weird. It may be the weirdest planet in the universe.

Yes, we've already found fifty three living worlds in this galaxy, and that in itself is pretty exciting, since we've only found seventy eight planets with life on them in our own galaxy in all the time we've been exploring it, and here we've found fifty three on our first expedition to this galaxy on our first visit here. But this weird world...

Like our galaxy, most of the planets and moons with life have only microbial life. We (well, the scientists, but they know what they're talking about) are certain that at least one of the many species on the planet is a tool-using species that has even constructed space vessels. We've never run across anything close to being like that, ever, in all the time our species has been exploring space.

I feel really honored to be the pilot of the first intergalactic vessel, even though we're visiting G2, the closest galaxy to our own. They're so close the two galaxies will eventually start to merge within our great grandchildren's lifetimes. But still, I'm the first one to pilot a craft out of the galaxy and into another one.

The really weird planet we found was the third planet from CXG-947. Okay, G2-CXG-947, but when I say CXG-947 you can assume the G2. Actually, you can assume all of them are G2 because that's where we were and all the stars are G2, just like our galaxy is G1.

Its surface is mostly dihydrogen monoxide like our planet, and unlike ours its atmosphere is mostly nitrogen. Most of the biologists were absolutely certain that life was impossible there, since there is so little free oxygen and carbon dioxide, but there it was. And not only life, but an incredible diversity of life, far more diverse than we've seen in any other life-bearing planet, in that galaxy or our own.

Ironically, the biologists weren't interested in the CXG-947 stellar system at all at first, as I said. They thought none of the planets' atmospheres or other environmental variables were fit for life.

The first planet from CXG-947 was small, hot, had no atmosphere, and one hemisphere always faced the star. The second had an atmosphere that was almost all carbon dioxide, and as a result was way too hot for life, as close as it was to the star. It would have been a perfect candidate for life if its orbit and the fourth planet's orbits were switched. The third had all that nitrogen, the fourth with almost no atmosphere at all, and all the other bodies were either too large or too small as well as being too far from the star.

It was the physicists who became interested in this star system first. They became curious when there was a short period where there were a number of flashes on XGC-947-3's surface that emitted radiation in a very wide spectrum, as if a miniature star had appeared and died on the planet's surface in an instant. This all happened on the planet's northern hemisphere thousands of times within a short ten lokfars, then stopped.

They wouldn't have even seen it were it not for luck. We were passing between XGC-947 and XGC-948 on our way to ODX-102 when the flashes went off. We were really close, and they wouldn't have seen them if we weren't. It was only by accident that we found this strange place.

More study revealed that the flashes were only semi-natural, that one of the planet's species had actually engineered them. They were the result of uncontrolled fission and fusion reactions on the planet's surface. The scientists have no idea why they did it, perhaps to test a scientific theory, or testing a means of harnessing those reactions' power and an accident happened, over and over. But they can only guess, and tell me they don't really know.

Life on this planet was unlike anything the biologists had imagined, starting with being able to live in all that nitrogen. Yes, nitrogen is inert, and that's the problem. Life needs oxygen or some other such highly reactive nonmetallic element, even if it's bound in a molecule like carbon dioxide, and so far oxygen and carbon dioxide were the only such gasses on planets that had anything actually living on them. However, the biologists tell me that perhaps there's a planet with an atmosphere of chlorine or some other highly reactive gas that bears life that we have yet to find. I'm only the pilot so I don't fully understand it like the biologists and chemists do, but that's what they told me.

Unlike any other life-bearing planet we've found, in our own galaxy or this one, some of its species are bipedal. Most of the bipedal animals the biologists studied were avian, but the intelligent species is also bipedal. I have no idea how anything could walk on only two legs, and the biologists are especially excited about it. Just try walking on two legs, it's impossible. Heck, just try standing on two legs without holding on to something! That would be worthy of a circus sideshow. It makes me chuckle just thinking about it.

But what fascinated the biologists the most was that none of the species were omnisexual. In every other planet we've seen, all species are, and any member of any species can impregnate any other member of the species, including herself. These strange animals only had one set of genitals each. Yes, it happens. Even in our own species there's an occasional child born with only one set of genitals, or worse and more rare two genitals of the same kind. But a planet where none of any of its animals have more than one set of genitals is unbelievably weird.

They're still trying to figure out how the intelligent species communicates, since so very few of the species there are bioluminescent, and the intelligent species isn't. The leading theory is some sort of telepathy. This theory seems to hold up because the physicists have detected minute amounts of electromagnetic radiation that seems to be mechanically produced transmitted in certain patterns. They're still trying to decipher the patterns, but so far haven't had any luck doing so.

Also, many species had strange projections from their... what the biologists call "heads". They think these projections, which biologists call "ears" have something to do with their telepathy. Still others suggest that a projection they've named a "nose" may have something to do with it.

Others have suggested that perhaps they are bioluminescent, only in a part of the spectrum we can't see. There are some species on that weird place that change color, and perhaps a tiny change of color is how the intelligent animals communicate.

The biologists wanted to land and do some up-close observations, but I vetoed that at once. The planet is simply too dangerous. There are violent animals, even the intelligent species, which sometimes cause huge explosions, and there are very often really nastily violent natural occurrences, such as high energy sparks hitting the ground from giant clouds of charged dihydrogen monoxide vapors, volcanoes, tornadoes, ground-quakes, tsunamis, and perhaps even scarier, more perilous things we hadn't yet witnessed. It's a very dangerous world, far too dangerous to land on. I had to explain to the biologists that landing there would be way outside the rule book, and if they kept pestering me I'd have to report them.

When the mini-stars were flashing on the planet's surface, the physicists sent a drone down for closer investigation, and it crashed. Those things never crash! And these mad scientists wanted to go down there? If they want to land they're going to have to find a crazier pilot than me.

There's so much to learn about this amazing planet. The biologists are especially excited. They keep eschewing the violence, saying we would be inedible to any life form there, but that's not enough for me. Not after that drone. And I wondered what "inedible" meant, but I didn't ask.

But we did fly really low sometimes. A few times, some machines tried to chase us. One seemed to shoot a rocket at us, but the rocket was really slow compared to us. That was another reason I refused to land, we simply didn't understand these creatures. The intelligent species had sent objects into the planet's orbit, and I kept our distance from those, too.

The biologists finally convinced me to allow a couple of drones to pick up a few species of one of the planet's life forms for study, all quadrupeds because the bipedal species were just too weird, and the hexapods and octopods were too small to handle easily or to study in any detail.

My veto of bringing up bipeds really upset the biologists, because they wanted to study these strange species badly. Strange? Lorg, they're downright weird. This whole gorflak planet is weird. Even the quadrupeds are weird; none of the quadrupeds have actimar limbs, although a few species sometimes use locomotive limbs for what animals on our planet would use actimars for, like picking stuff up. The intelligent bipeds and a few other species of bipeds do seem to have some sort of actimars, although they're nothing like any life on our planet's actimars.

A few weird species that seem to be related to, or at least similar to the intelligent species, live in large stationary life forms, don't seem to have locomotive limbs at all. Instead, they have four of those weird actimars that they use for locomotion. Great Gargoth, but the animals on that planet are unimaginably weird.

The biologists think that since they can live in all that nitrogen, maybe something can live in the liquid dihydrogen monoxide. I don't know, I'm no biologist but that makes absolutely no sense to me. How could anything breathe underwater? It's a crazy notion, if you ask me.

It seems that half or more of all of the species on the planet live by consuming other species. What horror! And what's even weirder and more disgusting than that, some species propagate their young by having some of their parts actually consumed by other species of organism, who excrete the young elsewhere. There are species living inside other species. This planet is beyond imagination weird. It gives a whole new meaning to the word "alien".

The periculumologists, who study security, said that the obviously sentient species should be exterminated, and perhaps other similar, semi-bipedal species that had actimars as well. They moved so quickly and seemed to advance their technology so rapidly that sooner or later they could reach our galaxy and would be a great threat to us.

The biologists nixed that idea, saying they posed no threat at all.

First, our planet is five times as massive as that one, and they could never land on our planet, or withstand the acceleration necessary for intergalactic travel in the first place. But more important was the seemingly short life span of the mobile species. They would never leave their galaxy and could pose no threat, violent as they were. They simply don't live long enough to ever reach us, even if they could stand the acceleration.

There were a few species that lived almost as long as your pet gorflag, and you know those don't live long, ten iglaps if you're lucky, but some stationary species that grew very large lived that long and are still alive. But no other species there comes close.

ODX-102 was supposed to be our last stop before returning, but they canceled that so they could study the wierdo planet more. I'm sure when the next expedition comes to G2 they'll be back to this crazy place. The other planets are similar to our galaxy's, but this crazy place was nothing like anything anyone had ever imagined.

Excitingly interesting as this weird planet is, I'm anxious to get home. It was a very long trip here and the trip back will probably seem even longer than it is. We leave in a single lokfar, and I should be home in about fifteen iglaps.

I don't know why I'm writing this, the messenger drone will only get there an iglap or two before I do, but I'm excited to be on this mission and I miss you all.

I managed to get a souvenir from the planet's satellite, which the sentient species visited a few times and apparently gave up on. The souvenir is about as weird as that whole planet.

Well, I have to start preparations for the journey back. I'll see you when I get there!

Dewey's War

"Hey, Ed! Haven't seen you in weeks. How are you? You look worried. The usual?"

"Hi, John. Yeah, and a shot of the strongest stuff on your shelf. I've had a really bad day."

"So what's wrong?"

"Trouble. And bad news for all of us Martians."

"Damn it, Ed, what's going on?"

"Earth's going on. I was in a teleconference with the other dome mayors all morning over it. We're in trouble. Earth is at war!"

"What? At war with who? Us?" John exclaimed somewhat ungrammatically.

"Each other."

"What? I thought it was a single government?"

"It was, sort of, although nations had a certain independence, but had to follow U.N. laws. North America, China, and Australia rebelled. The Arab states may be next. It's civil war!"

"So what's that got to do with us?"

"Trade, John."

"Oh, shit. I'd better call Dewey." Of course, he could only leave a message, since Mars and Earth were on opposite sides of the sun and the relay station was half an astronomical unit north of it, making radio lag even worse. It would be quite a while before the message reached its destination.

John left his message and got back to the mayor. “Okay, it affects me, but what’s it got to do with Mars? We can get along without Earth, we’re self-sufficient and have been for fifty years. I have a problem, some other Martians probably have the same or similar problems, but why does Mars have a problem?”

“Because technically we’re under the auspices of different states in the United Nations. We’re North American, the Alba Patera dome is Chinese. Half of the domes are European, so are affiliated with the U.N.”

“But we’re all *Martians*. I’m an immigrant, but most of us were born here and have never left the planet.”

“Half or more of the Euros here share that opinion, but their governments, like China’s and unlike ours and the Australians, are staffed with Earthians imported from Earth, and are appointed by Earthians rather than being elected by Martians.”

“How about the Africans and South Americans?”

“They’re neutral, but nobody from those continents have built domes here, anyway.”

“It it a hot war yet?”

“No, the diplomats are still talking but blockades are being erected. Give me another beer and another shot, John. This war crap is making me crazy. I just don’t know what to do.”

“Well, the only advice I have is to be nice to the European domes’ mayors, maybe try to talk up independence.”

“Independence?”

“Why not? We need to get untied from Mamma Earth’s apron strings. Why should we be tied to their laws? They’re millions of kilometers away!”

“You’re talking about revolution!”

“Yes, I am. Hopefully peaceful. But like I said, we have to follow a lot of laws and regulations that make perfect sense on Earth, but are either meaningless or downright stupid here. I think it's time!"

"John, that's crazy talk. We aren't even armed!"

"Yes, we are. You're forgetting who does half of all space transport, and that's Green-Osbourne Transportation Systems. Between the two of us, Destiny and I own a quarter of the company, and her dad and Charles control almost two thirds.

"We have the fastest, most heavily armed and armored ships in the solar system, and Dewey has worried about war for a long time and has been preparing. War's really bad for the shipping industry and we've always refused to engineer warships for Earth's governments just because of that. Not many people know it, but our transports *are* warships, and there aren't any Earthian government warships in deep space."

The Mayor sighed and ordered another beer and shot. "Maybe I should hold a Dome Hall meeting, televised and with the public invited so we can get a feel of the public's attitudes."

"Ed, better slow down on the alcohol. It wouldn't do to have a drunken mayor when war might be imminent."

"You're right, skip the shot but give me another beer."

"I agree about Dome Hall, but don't forget: GOTS is not about to let anything bad happen to Mars' colonies.

"Not only are we better armed, but we're experienced, thanks to the damned pirates. Dewey started the defense fleet eight years ago because of the pirates and we've killed or captured most of them. Earth's armies haven't any experience at all with real war; there hasn't been a shooting war for half a century except the war of shippers and pirates."

"Well, I don't know what to say."

"Say you're about drunk and it isn't even two in the afternoon and you need to go home and sleep it off."

"I'm not going to be able to sleep with this over my head!"

"Here, take these home with you," John said, pulling out a bottle of white lightning and a twelve pack of beer. "It wouldn't do to have the mayor staggering around the dome, especially now. Get drunk at home."

"You're right, of course... about getting drunk. But revolution?"

"Sleep it off and think about it. It's time Mars was independent. Look how much we're paying in taxes to Earth, and we're getting absolutely nothing from it. We could use that to make Mars a better place."

"I'll think about it."

"Look, Ed, stay sober tomorrow, okay?"

"I'll have to. See you, John."

"Later, Ed."

John's phone made a noise; there was a message from Dewey.

Aimée Beaulieu hated her job. She didn't want to be in this *damné* dome on this God-forsaken planet. But she had been exiled here; "exiled" isn't exactly accurate, but it's close.

She had been head of the EU's diplomatic corps, and had an idea that could give Europe more commercial power. She sent her diplomats to the other continents' governments with orders to negotiate her plan. Instead of negotiating, three of them, inexperienced but influential people appointed by Europe's government, presented the idea as an ultimatum.

They were fired and she was paying a price as well. Stuck on Mars, Mayor of one of the stupid domes.

Damned dome! She'd only been here a month and hated it with a passion. Now there was that stupid revolution, civil war, whatever back on Earth and they told her she was no longer allowed to trade with the North American, Australian, or Chinese domes.

And she loved Knolls beer, Damn it! That was the only good thing about this God-forsaken planet. She wondered what could be done about the situation. Probably nothing, she thought. Except by the idiots in charge on Earth, damn them.

She didn't much like the Martians, either, but she understood where they were coming from. A lot of the Martian-born Martians in her dome had been talking about independence from Earth. That would suit her... as long as she was off of this damned rock and back in France first. After all, if the dome revolted under her watch her career would be ruined even worse than it already was. She'd probably be forced to resign.

She sighed, and went back to the meaningless paperwork Earth demanded.

Chuck Watson, mayor of Ceres, was angry. What were those idiots on Earth thinking? If he followed their directive Cererians would surely starve! Those who had been born on Ceres had already been talking independence.

And Charlie, who had been a close friend for years and a trading partner for almost as long, he was prohibited from communicating with.

He had enough, he decided, and called Charlie. To hell with the Earthians!

Charlie Onehorse, Mayor of Dome Australia Two, was annoyed. DA2's main export, high quality steel and rare earth ferromagnetics mostly went to the European domes, and half of all the domes on Mars were European. And the ores were from the British mining colony on one of the asteroids. DA2 was going to have trouble both importing and exporting.

They could probably have ore shipped from China, but Earthian ores were incredibly expensive; mining anything on Earth was effectively outlawed by regulations that made it a hundred times cheaper to import from Martians and asterites. On top of this, ferromagnetics from the belt were a hundred times as strong as Earthian rare earth magnets.

He was thankful that a few of the North American domes were farming domes, since none of Australia's three domes had farms, and they had to import all of their food. He swore to himself that the situation was intolerable and would have to change.

Born in DA3, his parents were immigrants from Australia. His paternal grandfather had moved to Australia from somewhere in North America.

But unlike other countries' domes, the Australians had great autonomy. They could pass their own laws and regulations, and only had to pay tax to the Earthians. Still, paying those taxes rankled; the money would be better spent improving life on Mars. Things were still rough on the Martian frontier, although nowhere near as bad as it had been before the robot factories were built.

He wondered where the Europeans were going to get new robots, since the three robot factories were all in North American domes. Parts to repair malfunctioning robots, as well. He grinned at that, and thought to himself "bloody dills! Those bludgers are going to have to work now. Bloody hell, it'll be Rafferty's rules for sure; things are already becoming a bit chaotic."

He decided to call his old friend Ed Waldo. Ed always knew what to do when things got crazy.

Ed's secretary said he had taken the afternoon off.

"With this war stuff going on?"

"He said he was going to talk to his friend John, said John always knew what to do when things got crazy."

He should drop by Ed and John's dome and bend the elbow with them, he thought. He liked John, who didn't charge as much for his grog as anybody else charged for theirs, and his beer was the best. Even better than Victoria Bitter, although that brand's quality had suffered in the last couple of decades.

He called Ed's pocket number, but Ed had it shut off. He called the French dome, which was only twenty kilometers from DA2, but was told that there could be no communication with non-UN domes as well as no trade; the diplomats were all in charge. And there were no diplomats on Mars, only Earth.

Except, well, John, maybe. John wasn't even a real Martian. Not yet, anyway. You had to be a resident of any dome for ten years to get voting rights, even though those rights were pretty meaningless in some domes, like the Chinese and UN domes. John had two years to go before he was a citizen.

John had connections. He was the son in law of the founder of the biggest shipping company in the solar system, and he and his wife owned a quarter of company stock. He also had a small farm, a brewery, and a bar on Mars, all of which his wife said were hobbies even though they all made him a lot of money and even more friends.

As he was trying to figure out a plan, a message came from his friend and trading partner Chuck Watson. Luckily Ceres and Mars were close enough at the time that the radio lag wasn't too bad.

"Charlie, what are we going to do? The damned Earthians are killing us!"

"Come on, Chuck. don't over react."

"Charlie, I'm not. We're going to need food, where's it going to come from? Earth? We'll starve!"

"No you won't. Earthians can go to hell, we Martians and you asterites can stick together. You want to trade, we'll trade. We need rare earths and you need food, and neither of us needs Earth."

Of course, it was a very long conversation because of the lightspeed lag.

"You look like hell, Ed."

"Hung over, and I even had trouble sleeping after getting stumbling drunk. Got any coffee?"

"Yeah, coffee's free. The pot's over there."

"Thanks, John. What the hell am I going to do? We don't need much from the Europeans that the Chinese and Aussies can't provide, but if this lasts a long time..."

"Don't worry, it's only going to last a few months and when it's finished, Mars is going to be independent of Earth."

"No way. This is a diplomatic and economic war, it could last for years."

The mayor from the neighboring dome came in. "Hey, Charlie," Ed said. "Hell of a mess."

John grinned. "Nope. Where's Europe going to get any rare earth magnets, or any of the other rare earths?"

Charlie groaned. "John, ever hear of the asteroid belt?"

John grinned. "Yep. Ever heard of Green-Osbourne?"

"So what?"

"So they shouldn't have pissed off Dewey and Charles. First the Europeans seized company holdings in Europe, but luckily all the engineering is done in North America and most of the assets are in space. Then we lost a man and a landing craft when the Euros fired on it. It was full of my beer, too, damn it. Anyway, that was the last straw."

"I thought your ships were almost impervious to weapons?"

"Only the interplanetary ships. Landers and boosters have to deal with the gravity well and can't be that heavy."

"So what can Dewey do?"

"Guys, do any of you know anything about war?"

"I do," an elderly female voice piped up from the other end of the bar. "I was only twenty. It was horrible."

"Oh," said Ed, "Hello, Mrs. Ferguson. I didn't see you down there. Where are you going with this, John?"

"Earth hasn't had a shooting war for half a century, and their armies have forgotten how to fight. They're barely armies.

"Meanwhile, Mars has been at war almost from the beginning, at war with pirates. Green-Osbourne has an army, a space army, and an experienced one.

"Dewey convinced all the other shippers to refuse interplanetary shipments until the mess on Earth is over. Some he had to threaten, he made it clear that his army would allow no shipping, and people who tried to trade with Earth would be blown out of the sky. Nobody but Green-Osbourne is doing any shipping, and only to select clients, like us. You Aussies can have all the rare earths you can afford, but the Euros get nothing.

"China and North America are the only Earthly sources of rare earths, and there are no superferromagnetics on Earth at all, so Europe is screwed; mining is effectively impossible there. Their economies will collapse; they'll come around.

"Meanwhile, I expect to see riots in the European domes pretty soon. There will be revolution for sure. Lots of Martians are tired of being tied to Mother Earth's apron strings. We want to be free!"

"I don't know, maytie," Charlie said. "Australians almost have independence already, I don't see any revolt coming."

"John's right," Ed replied. "you folks will be last, except maybe the Chinese, you might revolt before them. But when we're not paying taxes to Earth and you are, and there's nothing that can happen to you for not paying the tax, you'll sign the declaration."

"Declaration?"

"We'll declare our independence. When the time is right. Mars has an army and Earth doesn't. They can't boss us Martians around any more!"

"Sir, we've detected a craft coming in from the belt."

"Very well, Captain Phillips. Disable it with an EMP and set it in orbit around Mars. It will be their prison until a treaty is signed, we'll supply them with the necessities of life."

"Yes, sir."

A month later, there was indeed rioting in the French dome. The elected, normally powerless city council presented a demand for independence from Earth; after all, Earth was powerless against Green-Osbourne, and that company had protected Mars from pirates—and now was protecting Mars from the Earthians.

The mayor refused to sign the declaration and was arrested, and an election for a new mayor was scheduled.

News reached the other domes, of course, and almost all of the Martians became rebels.

Three months later on June thirteenth, by Earth's calendar (Mars rotates at a different rate and is on a longer orbit), the UN had no choice but to sign a treaty with the Martians, which recognized the domes as sovereign states. Earth's economy was crumbling, citizens were doing more than grumbling, elected leaders were in danger of no longer being elected.

Earth no longer had the illusion of a single government.

Aimée Beaulieu was released from jail and returned to Earth after the treaty was signed, and retired with honors and a huge pension, seen as a patriotic hero by her French countrymen and the French government.

The only loss of life in the entire "war" was the Green-Osborne landing craft captain that the U.N. had shot down.

John's bar was full of happy people with nothing on their minds except celebrating Martian independence. John downplayed his involvement.

"I'm not even a real Martian, Charlie. Not for two more years. The real Martians, guys like you who were born here are the real Martians."

A voice came from a few stools down. "Hey John, don't you serve Frenchmen?"

"Lewis! Good to see you, old man. Lager?"

"Of course."

"So how do you like your new job?"

"Oh, man, I hate it. I wish I hadn't run for office, those damned Euros really fouled everything up. But I'll manage. Mars will, too, now that we're not wearing Earth's yoke."

"The second French revolution and nobody got guillotined!"

"The second American revolution, too. And it was a lot more like now than the French revolution."

John grinned. "I wouldn't know, my wife's the history buff. Excuse me, Lewis, it looks like there's a lot of empty glasses! PARTY!! Robot, don't just stand there, you stupid junkpile, get Lewis a lager."

Plutus' Revenge

It was the only life-bearing planet in the entire universe; the very first planet to have life. It was the only planet in existence to have the conditions necessary for biogenesis, including being a double planet, each orbiting each other. The double planet was one of the keys of biogenesis, because of the tides. The timing of orbits and gravities had to be perfect, as well as chemical and photonic conditions.

Life has a hard time getting started. This was the first planet on which it was possible. It would be billions of years before any other planet had these conditions.

In time, its rotation slowed as its sister planet Theia went farther away and took up an eccentric orbit around the star.

It was a very rich planet. Rich in metals, rich in diversity of vegetation once life had evolved that far, vast riches of water, and very rich in hydrocarbons. It was rich in chemicals and conditions conducive to abiogenesis. One of the planet's fauna evolved to the point of sentience, then the arts, than the sciences, until their technologies were very advanced. By the time this had come about, though, the slightly smaller sister had wandered away. The Vulcans never knew of it.

The Vulcans were a very religious people who worshiped Plutus, a god everyone could see and love. When the heretic prophet Ragnarok was twenty three, he warned them that Plutus had told him to inform everyone that he was commanding them to explore outer space, that there were vast riches there, and their very existence depended on it.

But space exploration isn't cheap, and the Vulcans couldn't see any monetary payback, only expense. Space travel wasn't started.

Fifty years later Ragnarok spoke of an evil that only Plutus could save them from, and said it was on its way, and called it Theia. He spoke before a crowd one day, saying Plutus had spoken to him in a dream. As they listened intently, he informed them that their god was angry because they had never left Vulcan and was going to destroy the Vulcans, and Ragnarok and his family were the only ones who would survive the cataclysm unless he told anyone of his dream, in which case he would die instantly and his family would perish as well. His blasphemy was met with a storm of stones, and he died there broken and bloody. The mob then murdered his family and set his house on fire.

But Ragnarok was right. The rich are never satisfied with their riches, so poured more and more of their seemingly limitless hydrocarbon riches into industry and commerce, all worshiping Plutus with all their hearts. Technology brought wealth, and was developed to a very high degree.

A century after the would-be savior Ragnarok was stoned to death, the Vulcan culture was already in decline. They developed space travel, but they never saw the signs of the decline. The denizens of a declining civilization never do. But space travel was developed despite its seemingly nonexistent to meager payoff, and a colony was planted on the next planet out from theirs, the third, and another on the fourth. The third planet was uninhabitable because of its almost completely nitrogen atmosphere, and space men and women had to wear oxygen masks and very heavy clothing outside. It was very cold there, having very low concentrations of greenhouse gasses. The planet was called "Schnee".

Schnee was the reason space travel was actually developed on Vulcan. Vulcan had been much like Raj a few centuries earlier, but had gradually warmed, becoming hotter and drier. The area near the equator become a desert with fewer and fewer forms of life, and its oceans started shrinking, the water entering the atmosphere as vapor and staying there. Collecting this water was very expensive, so they started looking at Schnee for water. It was a hard life for the scientists and ice miners there, many of whom froze to death.

The fourth planet, Raj, was much nicer. It had a nitrogen atmosphere with plenty of oxygen for animals to breathe, and carbon dioxide for plants to breathe and warm the planet, so had very comfortable temperatures near its equator. Scientists were there before too long, followed by rich tourists, followed by rich immigrants who went for its beautiful weather and the wonderful Marineris Ocean's seashores. As Vulcan became hotter, Raj became the star's ruling planet. All still worshiped Plutus.

Vulcan was dying, but wasn't yet dead when Theia returned. It had been in its eccentric orbit for billions of years, its orbit often changed drastically by a gas giant and a ringed planet.

Theia seemed to be headed directly to Raj! It came very close, its gravity from its larger mass than Raj's and its nearly all iron composition tearing away almost all of Raj's atmosphere. Animals, including the sentient Rajians whose ancestors had immigrated from Vulcan died in hours. Flora came to its end shortly later.

Raj's gravity altered Theia's course, and it was now headed directly to Schnee. Vulcan had fallen so far that its meager population of Vulcans had no idea of the destruction that had hit Raj, now dead, and what awaited Schnee. It mattered not to them, for they knew that they were doomed. Ragnarok's prophesy was well on its way to being true—but no one would be left alive to tell tales of the blasphemous prophet.

The Vulcans on Schnee saw Theia coming, but were helpless to do anything about it. There were few of them left, as well.

At first it was a white dot in the night sky that got brighter and brighter every evening, then bigger and bigger. Before long it was a huge circle. It hit Schnee with tremendous force, releasing tremendous energies. It made a giant splash of molten rock and metal, and steam from the suddenly boiled ice. Vulcans who still had binoculars could see rings around Schnee, but there were few Vulcans, let alone binoculars. They, the few animals, meager vegetation, and microbes in Schnee's atmosphere that had ridden to Schnee with the Vulcans were the only life in the entire universe.

Plutus had his revenge, making Vulcan so hot anything combustible burned, and soon there were rivers of flowing lead. Schnee was covered in an ocean of magma, and Raj was hit by so many meteors that all traces of Vulcan activity were erased completely. Plutus had not only destroyed the Vulcans, but all evidence of their very existence.

It was finally only the microbes in Schnee's atmosphere that lived, who had no way of appreciating the beauty of

Schnee's rings. Which was a pity, as they were very beautiful rings indeed.

Voyage to Earth

He awoke wondering where he was... on a medic. Why was... oh, hell, why was he being held down? And then the big question hit him—Who am I?

And who, besides the medic itself, which was only a robot, had imprisoned him? And why?

There was a tube leading into his arm... was he in a hospital? It *smelled* like a hospital.

The medic beeped, and said "condition improved, now stable."

He must have had some kind of accident, but he couldn't remember his own name, let alone how he wound up in a hospital.

"Computer!" he said, hoping the hospital computer could shed some light. It was apparently not paying attention, because it ignored him. He lay there strapped to the robotic table for what seemed like forever when the medic again beeped and spoke. "Condition improved, now fair."

"Computer!"

No answer.

Damn. "Medic!"

No answer.

Another eternity passed, and the medic reported "Condition good, patient released." The straps came loose and he sat up on the medic, waiting for a nurse or doctor that never showed up. Didn't someone have paperwork when a patient was released?

"How you been, old man?"

"Wild Bill! I haven't seen you since... damn. You haven't aged a day!"

"I've been in space, you quit. You know space travel slows aging. So how you been? I've been doing runs to Titan since the discovery."

"Bill, it's fantastic. My beer is the best selling beer on Mars, and they want us to export it to Earth. Can you believe it? And I have the cost down really low since I bought that warehouse to grow the ingredients in. I'm almost as rich as my wife!"

Bill laughed. "How is Destiny?"

"Oh, man, she's doing better than me. She's getting the damned Nobel Prize! She's going to be famous. I'm so damned proud of her!"

"Damn, that's hundreds of years old, not many prizes more prestigious than that. What did she get it for?"

"Her new telescope. She never told anybody but me, but her first PhD thesis was rejected; they didn't think her theory was sound. After she got her doctorate she decided to prove her theory and built that telescope here. The results were that her theory was on the money. They replicated it on the moon and got the same result and it was a huge paradigm shift in the astrophysics world. I'm really proud. So we're going to Earth. I'm taking a shipload of beer with me."

"Yeah, you always liked beer. I remember your last trip."

John laughed. "Fuck you, Bill, I'm not drinking it, I'm selling it. Earth is importing it from Mars."

"Earth is buying beer from Mars? Even with the shipping costs? What the forgswaggle?"

"Young man!" an old woman at the other end of the bar admonished, "Watch your fucking language, asshole!"

"Oh, shit, I didn't see you down there, Mrs... Ferguson, wasn't it? Terribly sorry, it won't happen again."

"I remember you, too, you foul mouthed asshole. Now watch your fucking mouth!"

"Yes, ma'am. John, Earthians are buying beer from Mars?"

John laughed. "Rich dumbasses trying to be cool. Mars is cool now, I could piss in a can and they'd buy it."

"I'm headed for Earth in a week, maybe I'll be your captain. When you leaving?"

"About a week. Hope you're running my load."

"Maybe I will. Hope so, anyway."

"Our friend Tammy's going, too. She's getting some kind of award for her work with the droppers and the discoveries she's made, although it isn't the Nobel. She found that Mars was perfect for curing dropheads; they hate low gravity when they're high, so being on Mars helps when they're withdrawing, as well as what she learned on the trip here."

"I don't think I met her when I was on your boat."

"Probably not, although she was probably watching you have fun with the whores. She never said anything about it, though."

"What??"

"She was studying them. Her research led to a cure for drop addiction, which is what her award was for. Her first success works for me now, she's the morning bartender. All of them are employed now, mostly in construction and robot repair."

"Is Mars still short of robots?"

"Not since that factory opened two years ago."

"I'm surprised you don't have robots tending bar, then."

"Screw that. People don't go to bars to drink, they go to bars to socialize; bars are full of lonely people. If there's nobody to talk to but a damned robot they're just going to walk out. I do have a tendbot for emergencies, like if one of the human bartenders is sick and we don't have anyone to cover. The tendbot will be working when we're going to Earth, but I avoid using it."

Bill took another sip of his beer. "How the hell did you learn to make such good beer, John?"

"Lots of books, lots of classes; I minored in chemistry, and lots and lots of trial and error."

"Well, I can sure see why you're exporting it. This stuff could make me an alcoholic! Damn but your beer is good," he said, draining the glass.

"Want another one?"

"Well, I was only dropping by to say 'hi' but this is some damned good beer. Yeah, one more and I have to go, but I think I'll take a case with me. Damn, but this is some good beer!"

An Asian woman walked in. "Lek!" John said. "Back so soon?"

"I forgot my purse," she said, retrieving it from a drawer behind the bar.

"Lek, Meet my oldest friend, Bill. Bill, Lek here is one of my best assets. She's been studying and knows five languages. That's a hell of an advantage in a Mars bar, since we get people from all over Earth coming here."

"Pleased to meet you, Lek. Where are you from? Chicago?"

She laughed. "No, but my English teacher was from Chicago. I'm from Bangkok."

"You really speak English good!"

John laughed. "Not so good when I first met her but you could understand her."

"It was nice meeting you, Bill, but I have to run, I have a class in half an hour. See you tomorrow, John."

"Oh, Lek, you're sure you don't mind doing the evening shift when I'm gone?"

"No, I told you, it's fine. Tips are better at night, anyway. See you!"

Bill said "Damn but this is good beer. Give me another one, John!"

He decided to look around the hospital to find someone and tell them that he shouldn't have been released, that he had no memory. He used the rest room and went searching for help.

This, he thought, was the strangest thing... this hospital seemed to have no doctors, no nurses, no administrative staff, nobody. Not even any patients. He walked down hall after hall, and found nothing but locked doors and more hallways.

He started to panic, and muscle memory reached his hand into his pocket for a phone. There was none there.

That panicked him even further. Why didn't he think of it before? It could have told him at least who he was, if not where he was and why.

He started running, down first one hallway then another, until he collapsed in exhaustion and anguish. He sat there in the hallway, head in his hands, sobbing softly.

Bill was, indeed, their captain. Of course, he was running a first class ship this load. First class ships had two dozen docks so passengers could take their own transportation with them if they so chose. John, Destiny, and Tammy took the houseboat up. A large chemical rocket took his huge load of beer up, enough to fill ten or fifteen railroad boxcars.

Bill met them at the dock, and John briefly introduced Bill to Tammy. Bill showed them their suites, and when the last of the half-dozen or so other passengers embarked and the robots finished moving John's huge load of beer, Bill left orbit.

After settling down in their quarters, John and Destiny decided to have lunch in the commons. There was a very large, scary looking black man in a business suit sitting at the bar and sipping a martini. He took notice when they walked in.

"Excuse me, sir," the large fellow said, "Are you John Knolls?"

"Yes, sir," John replied. "And you are...?"

"Dick Martin, Mister Knolls. I love your beer! My houseboat's half full of your beer, you can't get beer as good as yours on Earth!"

"Well, thank you, Mr. Martin. What do you do?"

"I'm an engineer. I work for this shipping company. Had to go to Mars to oversee the installation of some equipment I designed. Sure will be glad when I get back to Earth!"

John laughed. "I'll probably be glad to get back to Mars. After ten years of Martian gravity I'm going to hate Earth."

Martin laughed. "I probably won't much like it after two months on Mars, either. I'm sure not looking forward to the centrifuge. But I'm looking forward to getting back, they have a new toy I want to play with."

"They didn't tell you? We'll be at over a gravity by the time we reach Earth."

"Really?"

"Yes, between the two of us my wife and I hold nearly a third of the company's stock. We can pretty much do as we please. It probably won't take a week to get there. So, what kind of toy?"

Dick grinned. "Company toy. We're getting some of those new molecular printers, can't wait to try it out."

"Molecular printer?"

"Yes, it's a printer that builds objects molecule by molecule. You can get some pretty wild stuff from it. I feel like a kid at Christmas!"

Destiny had ordered pork steaks, fried potatoes, broccoli, and green beans cooked with pork bacon. "John," she said, "The food's here."

"It was nice meeting you, Mr. Martin. Please excuse me."

The large man went back to his cocktail and John sat down with Destiny as a portly, shabbily dressed, nerdy looking young man came in frowning, and ordered a double whiskey from the tendbot.

John and Destiny finished their lunch, John remarking that those were the best green beans he'd ever eaten.

Destiny laughed. "It's the pork bacon."

Pork was incredibly expensive because of Earth's environmental regulations.

"Those pork steaks were pretty good, too," John said. They had coffee and pie, and went back to their quarters. Destiny put on a new holo and they watched it, drinking Knolls' Stout Lager.

They had dinner in their suite, and went to the commons for cocktails. Destiny ordered a zinger splash, and John ordered a Knolls lager.

The nerdy looking fellow fell off his stool as Bill came in. "God damn it," he said, "this is why I hate passenger runs. At least the damned drunk didn't start a fight." He called a medic to take the drunk to his quarters.

"Hi, guys," he said to the Knolls. "Destiny, John tells me you're getting the Nobel Prize! Is he bullshitting me?"

Destiny laughed. "No, he's right. We're going to Stockholm."

"Man, that's great," he said. "You must be really proud!"

Tammy walked in as Destiny said "Well, duh! Jesus, Bill, it's the Nobel!"

John laughed. "Told you, asshole. I wouldn't shit you about anything like that."

"Hi, guys, Captain. What's up?" Tammy said.

"Tammy, Captain Kelly here is my oldest friend. We went to high school together. Bill, this is our good friend Tammy Winters. I think you met her at the dock. I've known her for ten years or so and she and Destiny have been friends since college. She's a scientist, too. She's going to Sweden for the Rudolf Virchow Award."

"Congratulations, uh, Doctor? What's that award?"

Tammy smiled. "Just Tammy, Captain. It's for my research in prostitute communities. It took the anthropology world by storm, but not near as big a storm as Destiny's telescope caused!"

"Wow, you guys are going to be famous!"

Tammy laughed. "Destiny will, I'll just make the other anthropologists jealous. I'm getting an APA, too, but you don't get famous for those, either. Where's that waiter? WAITER!"

Destiny laughed. "Yeah, I'll be famous for fifteen minutes."

A waiter came over apologizing profusely. John frowned. Tammy ordered. John said "I hate those damned talking robots, glad I'm not running these boats any more. Do they all talk now, Bill?"

"Yeah, most of them. Especially on passenger boats. Another reason I like cargo runs."

The large black man walked in. John waved, and he walked over. "Hi, Mister Martin," John said.

"Call me Dick, sir."

"Don't call me sir, call me John!"

Dick smiled, and asked "Did that jerk leave?"

"What jerk?" Bill asked.

"Fat dorky looking guy that was in here earlier. My God but he was annoying."

Bill said "Well, if it's the guy I think you're talking about, he passed out. A medic rolled off with him."

A thin, attractive black women walked in. "Oh, excuse me, folks," Dick said, and walked over and met the woman.

An elderly lady entered. “Uh, oh,” John said. “Mrs. Ferguson. You’re in trouble, Bill. I wonder why she’s going to Earth? And how she got a first class ticket?”

Mrs. Ferguson spied Bill, frowned, and walked over. “Well, if it isn’t the asshole with the foul mouth! They’re letting a dickhead shitmouth like you be captain?”

“I watch my language when I’m on duty, ma’am. I’m sorry I offended you.”

Dick called out from the next table, “Blagger off, you busdown forgswaggled fognart!”

The old woman got a disgusted look on her face and left in a huff. Everyone burst out in riotous laughter. Bill shook Dick’s hand and bought him and his wife a drink. They were all becoming a little intoxicated. Another couple and a single man came in, but by then they were too drunk to worry about, or be able to remember, names anyway.

It had started to become sort of a party, but Bill and Tammy seemed to be hitting it off, and since ten years later John and Destiny still felt like they were on a honeymoon, went home to cuddle to a movie, cuddle to twentieth century music, and go to bed.

Quite a while later he finally came to his senses, sort of. He got up and decided to just walk around, looking for... anything, really, but especially people. Where was everyone? It would be nice if he could find a sandwich, too; he was starting to get a little hungry. That added to his already numerous worries.

He found no exits, no unlocked doors, no people, no sandwiches. It was hard enough to keep his fear below panic levels, but then what was obviously some sort of alarm went off. Was the building on fire? He stopped, with no idea what to do.

He looked up—weren’t there skylights showing stars earlier? But his memory was impaired, after all, not able to remember his name or anything before waking up on the medic.

He heard the first sounds that didn't come from robots that he'd heard since awakening, and it scared him even more —the sound of hail. Perhaps there were skylights, but were now shuttered.

At this point he was aware that the alarm was almost certainly a tornado warning, and he couldn't find the stairway! Maybe this building didn't even have a basement, but who in their right mind would build a structure in a tornado zone without one? But without a stairwell, it might as well not have a basement. He huddled in a doorway waiting for the tornado to destroy him and the building.

"Pork sausage again? You said it made you feel guilty!"

Destiny smiled. "I told you, it's because I'm frugal. Tammy says I might be nuts. But this is paid for, part of a first class ticket!"

John laughed. "Tammy's right. You're nuts!"

Destiny grinned and dug into the ham and cheese omelet with a side of pork sausage.

Bill's eight o'clock adjustments needed no adjusting, and he wondered if the whole trip would be this easy. After all, it was only going to take a little more than a week, since their gravity would have increased to one point four before they docked, and Mars and Earth were pretty close right now.

John and Destiny were coming out of their suite as he was inspecting that section. "Bill," John said, "you look like hell!"

"Man, I am so damned hung over... man. Me and Tammy sure tied one on. Damn, but I like that woman! Uh, don't tell her I said that."

John laughed. "She has PhDs in psychology and anthropology, dumbass. She already knows."

"Well, shit!"

Destiny laughed. "Don't worry, Bill, Tammy studies what she studies because she loves people and studies how to make them hurt less. She'd never hurt you on purpose, and I'd bet she knows you better than you know yourself. Doing inspections?"

"Yeah."

"We're just going for a walk. Want some company?"

"Sure, but I can't let you downstairs. John knows that." They were walking past the cargo area.

John and Destiny both started laughing. "What's so funny?" Bill asked, perplexed.

"You!" they both said in unison. John added, "Computer: open C-17." The door opened.

"What the..." Bill started. "What... Damn it, John, how in the hell did you do that?"

Destiny laughed. "Bill, only my dad and Charles have more stock in this company than John and I do. We own the damned ship. But to tell you the truth, I really don't want to go up and down five flights of stairs."

John laughed. "That's one reason I retired. I hated those God damned stairs! Hey, come in here, I opened the door to show you something."

"You opened the door to freak me out!"

"Yeah, but I still want to show you something. My new cans and bottle labels." He opened a case and handed a can to Bill.

"Knolls' Martian Ale? Funny name for a lager."

John laughed. "I don't just make lager. So what do you think about the new design?"

"I don't know. Why is Mars white?"

"Because it's ale. Lager is green and pilsner is red."

"Why?"

"You going to pay me tuition? Look it up."

Bill laughed. "Asshole," he said. "Going downstairs?"

Destiny said "I don't think so" in almost unison with John, who instead said "No fucking way in hell!"

Bill's alarm went off. "God damn it," he said."

"What's the problem?" Destiny asked.

"I can't talk about it. John knows that."

Destiny laughed. "You work for me, Bill. I can fire you, you know." He looked at John, who said "It's okay, what's the danger?"

"A pirate." John and Destiny looked at each other. "A pirate?" John asked.

Bill shook his head. "Beats the hell out of me, that's what the computer said." They all went to the pilot room.

Bill sat in the pilot seat. It looked like the pirate was trying to communicate. There was only one ship, which puzzled all of them. Bill let him communicate.

"Stand and deliver!" the pirate ordered. All three burst out laughing. "What the hell does that mean?" Bill said, and pressed a button. "What do you want, dumbass?"

"You will surrender your ship or be destroyed!"

All three laughed even louder; these ships were nearly impervious to weapons, especially the weapons available to pirates. An atomic explosion couldn't even damage it unless it detonated less than two hundred meters away, and the pirates had no atomics.

"Do your worst," Bill told the pirate, laughing.

Lasers and chemically propelled projectiles rained on the ship, of course with no effect. "Should I kill him?" Bill asked. It would have been easy.

"No," John said, "Kill his ship, hit it with an EMP and have the company come out and snag his ass. That boat is surely stolen, the company might make some cash and you might get a raise."

"I don't know," Bill said. "Bastards have killed our friends."

"Everybody dies," John said. "Not everybody spends their life in prison before they do. Give him an EMP, lots worse than an atomic, and you might get a raise. And he might run out of air or freeze to death before security reaches him."

Bill disabled it with an EMP and called the company. The three of them started towards the commons for a cup of coffee before Bill finished inspections when another alarm went off.

"Damn it," Bill said, pulling out his phone. "Ladies and gentlemen, your attention, please. We will be experiencing lowered gravity for a short while. Please excuse the inconvenience." The three of them walked back to the pilot room, and Bill slowed the ship down.

Suddenly Bill said "Holy shit!"

"What?" John asked.

"There's a ship headed right for that meteor shower we slowed down for, and he's really hauling ass! It's one of ours," he added. "Didn't see it until he passed us, he's in full stealth mode."

The sounds of hail stopped, the siren stopped, and yes, there were skylights; the shutters opened then, showing stars once again. Odd that the storm had started and ended so fast. The shutters must have closed before the clouds rolled in.

He started to continue his fruitless search.

A robot wheeled past, and he had an idea. The robot would certainly lead him to *something.*

It did. Down a hallway he'd not yet explored and probably had run past more than once in his earlier panic was a large door that stood wide open, the automatic pocket doors recessed. Inside was a huge room filled with tables and chairs, but still no sign of humanity at all. The robot he'd followed dragged another robot away. Puzzling.

At least he had somewhere to sit besides the floor. He sat down at one of the many tables to rest, thinking he'd have to figure out how to find his way back before continuing his search.

He just couldn't stop wondering what the hell was going on. Was he being studied in some sort of weird experiment?

Was he a prisoner by design, or by accident? Was he a criminal? Did he have a family?

Without even thinking he started praying out loud, "Oh, Lord, please help me..."

A mechanical voice chimed in. "Can I help you, sir?"

He looked up at the robot. "Yes," he said, "how can I get out of this building?"

"I'm sorry, sir, but that is not in my database. Can I get you something to drink?"

"Yes, cold water, but first, where am I?"

"This is the commons area, sir. Would you like a menu?" Without waiting for an answer, the video screen displayed a menu.

"Yes, I'll have a cheeseburger, brogs, and a caffeine shike."

"Yes, sir," it said, and started to roll away.

"Wait!" the man said. "What is this the commons of?"

"That information is not in my database."

"Can you tell me what this building is?"

"I'm sorry, sir, but that information is not in my database. Is there anything else, sir, or shall I fetch your order?"

"No, go on." It rolled off. He put his elbow on the table and rested his head in his hand.

The robot came back shortly with his water and shike and rolled away again.

"What the hell is going on?" he wondered aloud, again.

The robot came back in with his food and wheeled away. He ate, still not able to figure out how to examine his prison and still find his way back to this "commons". At least he had food and drink now, which relieved him greatly and made exploration of this building far less, yet still, important.

Then he thought: A *commons.* A common area. People should show up here, perhaps he should just wait for someone to show up?

Several hours later and the skylight still showed stars. Was he in Antarctica? Or was he... Yes, that explained everything. He was on a space ship, but why? Where was it going? Where was the captain?

Was *he* the captain? Or... a horrifying thought came to him. Was he a pirate who had killed the captain and thrown the body out of the airlock?

"Damn it," John said. "What the hell is wrong with its captain? Pirates got him?"

"One of our ships? Not very likely," Bill said.

"It must be. Why would that captain drive right into a rock storm?"

They watched the computer display in horror as the other ship went through the rocks. Bill spoke on the phone again, alerting the company about what had just happened. When the meteor shower passed, he sped the ship back up and they headed to the commons for their delayed coffee.

Tammy was in there with coffee and a stylus tablet, so they started to join her, but the obese drunk, now sober, walked up and said "Excuse me, Captain..."

"Yes?" Bill answered.

Bill saw the big knife way too late and found himself on the floor, bleeding from the abdomen.

"I'm the captain now," the fat man said, waving the big bloody blade. "Nobody but me can get you to Earth alive."

"Think so?" Tammy said. "Think again." She kicked the knife out of his hand as a medic swiftly wheeled in, then she whirled around and kicked him in the head. He went down hard.

John was tending to Bill, and took his taser and handcuffs. Dick walked in with his wife as the medic rolled off with Bill, Tammy following.

"Oh, my God!" Dick exclaimed. "What happened?" John was cuffing the portly fellow. Another medic wheeled up.

"That asshole tried to murder my best friend," John said.

Dick was wide-eyed. "We're in trouble. How will we get to Earth without a captain?"

"Don't worry," John said, "I ran boats like this one for a quarter of a century.

Dick gave him a puzzled look. "You can't be much older than thirty."

John laughed. "Space. Times on a boat are different than standing still time, I'm almost fifty. We'll be fine. Look, Dick, I have to make sure that asshole pirate is locked up and see how bad off Bill is." He went to sick bay while Destiny took over assuring passengers in the commons that everything was going to be all right.

The flabby man was strapped firmly to the medic. Bill was pale, but awake. Tammy was there with him. John asked "How did you do that, Tammy? That was amazing!"

She grinned. "Lek gave me lessons, said she owed it to me for curing her drop addiction. I never thought I'd have to use it!"

Bill groaned. "John, what am I going to do? I have to get us to Earth, but it's going to be a while before I can get out of bed."

"Tell the computer to transfer control to me and I'll take care of it. And the paperwork."

"God, John..."

"Forget it, Bill. I want to get us there in one piece, too. Just get your rest and I'll take care of things until you can get around again."

Bill asked "What the hell was that guy's problem?"

John shook his head. "Fucking pirate. Another one. I'll question him when he wakes up. Look, I'm going to the pilot room to send paper and look at your schedules. I'll come back as soon as I can."

His thoughts were interrupted by the sounds of humanity—boots walking down the hallway, and cautious whispering voices.

He looked around the doorway and saw ten heavily armed, armored, and helmeted men.

"Oh shit," he thought. He was captain, but didn't even recognize his own boat, let alone how to run it, and now there were pirates who would surely murder him and steal the ship and whatever cargo it was carrying. He cowered in a corner, wishing for something to defend himself with.

They came in, weapons drawn, with the men in the back facing the other way and backing in. The man in front lowered his weapon and raised his face shield. "Jerry? Christ, man, what the hell is going on?"

"My name is Jerry? Are you sure? I don't know who I am!"

"Jesus, Jerry, I've known you for years, you're Jerry Smith. I was scared shitless for you, what the hell happened? Did you get attacked by pirates?"

"I... I don't think so. I'd be dead if they had. The first thing I remember is waking up on a medic wondering who I was and where I was and why I was on a medic. I wandered around for hours, I don't think anybody else is here."

"Okay, Joe, check the pilot room. Rob, would you do an engine inspection?"

"Sure thing, boss."

"Jerry, where are your phone and tablet?"

He shook his head. "No idea, but I was sure wishing I had them."

They took Jerry to Earth with them while another man piloted Jerry's ship there.

"Look, Mrs. Ferguson, everything will be all right!"

"But Miss..."

"It's Doctor, Ma'am. Doctor Knolls. It will be okay! Really!"

"Doctor? You don't look like a doctor. But there isn't anybody to run the ship!"

"I told you John was a captain in this very company for over two decades, and he was the best. There's nothing to worry about."

"Well, frankly, 'Doctor', I'm afraid I simply don't believe you. John's been tending that bar for years and just isn't old enough to have been a captain for that long. For that matter that foul-mouthed captain that got hurt is barely old enough to be a captain. And how long have you been in practice, 'Doctor'?"

Destiny laughed. "I'm not that kind of a doctor, I'm an astrophysicist. A scientist. And John's a whole lot older than he looks because he spent half his life in space. The faster the ship goes, the faster time goes outside the ship as far as the people inside are concerned. He and Captain Kelly are both almost fifty; they went to high school together. They just look young, John's fifteen years older than me but he doesn't look it."

"Well," the old woman said dubiously, "At least he doesn't have a foul mouth. At least he's a gentleman. I sure hope you're not lying to me, young lady!" she added sternly, with a glare. "Where is he, anyway?"

"Questioning the would-be assassin."

"Well, thank you, I guess. Bartender! Another martini, you mangy metal monstrosity!"

"Here you are, ma'am," the robot said, handing her the drink.

"Fuck off, junkpile. God, but I hate talking robots!"

Destiny laughed. "So does John. Robot, give me a Knolls Ale and shut up."

"I always did like that boy. He's really a captain?"

"Yes. Over twenty years."

"He's really fifty?"

"Yes, like I said, space travel."

"Gee, I should have been a captain!"

Destiny laughed. "You still live the same number of years, your time. It's just that when you travel, more time passes on the planets than you experience."

Mrs. Ferguson shook her head. "That relativity stuff is over my head."

"How are you feeling, Bill?"

"Better than I was before the robot did surgery. I still hurt like hell. Is my ship all right? Did the pirate wake up?"

"Yeah, she's fine, just did inspection for you. Everything's shipshape despite our acceleration. Surprising."

"They're doing a lot better job of designing and building these things than when you were captain. If that had been an old boat that went through those meteors it would have surely been destroyed, and it's been years since one of the robots or wall panels caught fire. I'm worried about engine forty two, though, watch that one close."

"Why? What's wrong with it?"

"Do you know how an ion engine works?"

"No."

"Well, I can't explain it to you then, but the wiring looks different than the wiring on the other motors. It worries me, I wish I was an engineer. I'm afraid that if we shut it down it will explode."

"What?"

"Like I said, I'm not an engineer but I can read a schematic, and since you don't know how they work I can't explain it, but it looks to me like they screwed up the wiring. Is the pirate awake?"

"Yeah, and I wasn't the least bit nice to the asshole. He spilled, though. Seems that he was in cahoots with the pirate you disabled; that guy was early, or Skankley was late."

"Skankley?"

"His name, Robert Skankley. He was supposed to take over the ship before the other pirate engaged, and the two of them would lock up the passengers in the other boat and either collect ransom or work them to death.

"You were targeted because of Destiny; Dewey would have paid a king's ransom to get us back.

"Stupid pirates. How long is the medic going to keep you here?"

"It says sometime tomorrow, but I'll be restricted to light duty. You'll still have to do downstairs inspections for me."

"Damn. I wish we hadn't ordered full gravity."

"You'll be glad when you get to Earth and don't need the centrifuge. I wish we had an engineer."

"I guess. But we do have an engineer, Dick."

"Who?"

"Dick Martin, the big black fellow. He's an engineer for the company but I don't know what his specialty is. I'll talk to him. I'm going to go to the commons and see if I can do anything helpful there; they're sure to worry since you're stuck in sick bay. If Dick's in there I'll talk to him. Call if you need anything."

"Thanks, John."

"Don't mention it."

John could see why Bill was worried; you would expect all the wiring on all the motors to be identical. When he reached the commons, the passengers were already calm, even having a good time. Almost all the passengers were drinking and laughing, and he saw no sign of unease at all. Destiny and Tammy were sitting at a table. He walked up and sat down. "I expected everyone to be worried, considering what happened tonight."

"It was Tammy," Destiny said. "That's her field."

Tammy laughed. "It was gin. I couldn't do anything with Mrs. Ferguson, but she listened to Destiny. At least after a few martinis."

They chatted a while, and Tammy went to visit Bill in sick bay. John and destiny had two more drinks and went back to their cabin.

The next morning John did Bill's eight o'clock pilot room duties, and as he headed past the commons on his way downstairs, he spied Dick standing by the bar drinking coffee, and sauntered over to talk to the large black man. "Excuse me, Dick."

"Hi, John, what's up?"

"Uh, its..." he looked around. "Kind of... can I talk to you in private?"

Dick frowned. "Sure." They walked out to the hall. "You said you're an engineer for the company, what kind of engineer?"

"Electrical, why?"

"Because Bill says the wiring on engine number forty two is different than all the other engines."

"Oh, my God!" Dick exclaimed. He would have gone pale if his skin could have allowed it. "A Richardson Death Ship! We need to have everyone evacuate to their houseboats immediately and sit tight there."

"What?!" Exclaimed John.

"No time, give the order to the passengers and I'll explain."

"Okay." John spoke into his phone. "Attention, passengers. An emergency has arisen aboard ship. Please evacuate to your houseboats and wait there until things are normal. We apologize for the inconvenience. Thank you. Captain Knolls out.

"So what's wrong, Dick?"

"Ten years ago, an electronics hobbyist was Mr. Osbourne's intern. He found a schematic wiring diagram that was wrong, and showed it to his boss, the company president. Well, the chief technical officer and five engineers got fired for that bad schematic, and rightfully so.

"It was wired into ten ships, all of which had to be rewired. Every single one of those three hundred ion engines on each of the ships. We worried that someone would miss an engine and they'd have a death ship. You might make a hundred runs, but sooner or later that thing's going to blow. And when it's shut down is when it will blow.

"We called this model the 'Richardson Death Ship'. This ship is one that had to be rewired, and it looks like they missed a motor."

"But these things will take an atomic!"

"That's why it's so dangerous in here and safe in the houseboats. When that engine blows, all the force will be inside the ship; outside will be fine except right outside the docks by storage; we'll open the inside door to the airlock and if it blows, the force will go there rather than to houseboat locks."

"Let's go talk to Bill."

"You should evacuate until I can study the schematics and see if I can rewire it while it's running."

"No, I can't. I'm captain until Bill's back on his feet. Come on."

An hour later, Dick met Bill and John in the sick bay, where the robot was just releasing Bill for light duty. "I can fix it," Dick said. "I'll need some wire and alligator clips, and a wire cutter."

"They're by each generator, forty two is closer to port. I'll show you."

"No, you and Bill better get to safety. No sense anybody but me gets killed."

"No," John said. "I'll help. Bill, wait in your boat. How long will it take you, Dick?"

"Maybe an hour. There's nothing you can do to help, and it's incredibly dangerous."

"I can hand you tools. That's an order. Come on."

The medic Bill was on rolled to his houseboat, and John and Dick climbed down into the bowels of the giant ship. John was indeed helpful and it only took forty five minutes. Dick stood up and brushed himself off. “Okay, you can shut it off now and I’ll take the board out, and the passengers can Re-embark.”

“We can shut it down from here,” John said, and did so. He addressed the public address, telling passengers they could come back on board, that the situation was resolved. He and Dick trudged up the steps at almost Earth gravity.

“I hope I’m getting paid for this!” Dick said, panting.

“Yeah, you’re getting paid. And you’re getting a raise, too.”

“How do you know?”

“I’m on the board of directors.”

“Oh.”

“Look, Dick, everybody’s going to want to know what’s going on, explain it so they don’t really understand but are calmed down and satisfied.”

Dick grinned. “I can do that.”

“Dick, you’re a hero, you know. I’m buying you a drink when we get to the commons!”

Dick shook his head. “I’m no hero, it’s just that I’m the only guy who could do it.”

“Bullshit, you could have waited in your houseboat while I played Russian roulette in the pilot room shutting that damned engine down, but you risked your life. That makes you a hero.”

“John, you were there, too.”

John shrugged. “Nah, part of what a ship’s captain is paid for is hazardous duty. I’m used to it, did this for more than twenty years. Uh, please don’t let the other passengers know how much danger we were all in.”

Dick laughed. “I know company policy, don’t worry.”

They reached the commons and John asked Dick what he was drinking. Dick shrugged. “Martini, I guess.”

A robot wheeled over. “What would you gentlemen like?” it asked.

John answered “A martini and a Knolls stout lager, a shot of bourbon and for you to shut up, you metal monstrosity.”

Dick laughed. The robot said to him “And what would you like, sir?”

“God damn it, you stupid pile of wires, the martini is for him and I told you to shut up. Now shut the fuck up and get us our drinks and I don’t want to hear another word from you.”

The robot rolled rapidly away and Dick said “I hate talking robots, too.”

“Almost everybody does. Somebody should talk to engineering, I guess.”

“John, I *am* an engineer and *I* hate ‘em. But management wants to show off our superior technologies.”

Bill came in on his medic, now folded into a chair shape. “Hi, guys. Damned robot won’t let me walk.”

“Well, you probably shouldn’t, then,” John replied.

“I hate taking orders from a damned robot,” Bill growled. “Where’s that damned bartender? I could really use a shot and a beer right now.”

Others started in, and Dick got busy confusing the other passengers with what folks outside the technical fields call “technobabble”. The robot finally returned with the drinks, and Bill said “What took you so damned long, junkpile?”

The robot turned its camera towards John and froze. “Robot?” Bill said. “Bartender!”

But the bartender wasn’t going to move; lights weren’t even shining. It stood there like a statue. “Must have broke, maybe its battery or something came loose,” Bill said.

“Fuck it,” John said, “I’ll tend the God damned bar. Call for a server, would you?”

Dick had joined the others at the bar, speaking the engineer’s perplexingly complex jargon and baffling everyone, all but Mrs. Ferguson pretending to understand. “Damned kids today, they just don’t talk the same language!”

John walked around the bar as Destiny and Tammy came in. Destiny laughed. “Told you so,” she said. “He loves tending bar!” She walked around and kissed him.

“Damned robot broke, Bill’s calling a repairbot.”

Dick looked at the dead robot and said “That’s an R 15 XB. A repairbot can’t fix those.”

“Why not?”

“They’re brand new, I didn’t even know we had them in deployment and can’t figure out why they did, because the repairbots haven’t been fully reprogrammed yet. I’ll look at it.”

His wife laughed. “Dick’s happiest when he’s up to his elbows in wiring,” she said. “John reminds me of him.”

Dick tinkered with the robot while John tended bar and everyone else drank and chatted. Finally Dick walked back to his stool while the robot wheeled around to the other side of the bar. “Cool,” John said. “What was wrong with it?”

Dick snickered. “It’s a safety bot. Brand new and more bugs than a picnic.”

“Safety bot?” Mrs. Ferguson asked. “Oh, hell, why do I bother?”

“Well,” Dick began, “hundreds of years ago there was this guy named Asimov who wasn’t even an engineer, but was a biochemist who wrote fiction on the side. Well, this guy coined the word ‘robotics’ and dreamed up what he called the ‘three laws’. It was all fantasy, when he wrote it there were no robots and computers were brand new and so primitive they weren’t really computers, but some people called them ‘electronic brains’. This guy had his robots run by positronic brains.”

“So what’s this guy’s fiction got to do with that bartender?”

“The ‘laws’ were safety devices, and the company has been trying to program something similar into our robots. From what I could gather, this one had two conflicting demands and couldn't cope and just shut down. I did a system reset and it's fine. Guess I should file a bug report."

He sat down with the captains and the scientists and ordered a drink from the server. "You told the robot to shut up, and the captain here told it to talk. It's easy to fix, there's a reset button right inside the panel. You'd think they could have programmed the repairbots to push the damned button when they couldn't figure it out.

"Programmers... they need to learn engineering. Or maybe psychology. They should at least learn how a computer works, but I don't think they teach that in programming school."

Bill said "The stupid robot should be able to figure it out."

Dick grinned and shook his head. "Robots can't think."

"But they're networked with the computer, and it can figure ship trajectories. I can't do that. They have encyclopedic memories, I don't."

"Do you know what an abacus is?"

"Of course, they used them thousands of years ago to do simple arithmetic."

"So how many beads would it take for it to become intelligent?"

"I don't get it."

Mrs. Ferguson, sitting at the bar, overheard. "Well, at least I'm not the only one. How can something with that much knowledge be so stupid?"

"I get it," Destiny said. "They used to have non-electronic books. Before there were computers, books were just lots of sheets of paper with information printed on them, bound together. A book held encyclopedic memories but had no memories of its own."

"Exactly. As to how it does calculus, it's pretty much done like an abacus works. Ever heard of a slide rule?"

John shook his head. "Nope."

Destiny said "I do. They looked like measuring rules, but there was an inside part that slid and a clear piece. Line the numbers up right and it would do multiplication, division, logarithms, all kinds of math. Engineers used them before they had computers."

"That's right, and a computer doesn't know that two times two is four any more than a slide rule does. When you tell it to tell you two times two, it takes the binary number two and shifts it to the left."

"I don't get it," Mrs. Ferguson said.

"Neither do I," John agreed.

"I'll show you how to do binary arithmetic some time," Destiny answered. "I had to learn it for that telescope. Speaking of which, will we be turning around in a couple of days, Bill?"

Somebody called out from the bar "the bartender quit again."

"Damn it," Dick said. He reset the robot and told it "Robot, do not talk. If someone asks you a question, display the answer on your screen. Do you acknowledge?"

The screen flashed "yes".

"Stupid programmers," Dick said.

Bill finished his beer and said "well, I'd better call it a night." Everyone else partied on.

The next day was "turnaround" day, when the ship turned around and used its thrusters as brakes; they were two thirds of the way there by now, three days into the trip, and traveling at fantastic speeds. They would reach Earth two days later.

Bill was healing rapidly, thanks to the healing drugs that had been developed a century earlier. No longer confined to a wheelchair, he was using a cane to get around. He met John, Destiny, and Tammy for breakfast after his eight thirty chores in the pilot room.

"Did you guys order yet?"

"No," John said. "We waited for you. Robot!"

"Yes sir?" the contraption said. "Are you folks ready to order?"

"Yes," John said, "I'll have scrambled eggs, toast, bacon, and hash browns and you'll just shut up and bring our food when the rest have ordered. I want no noise from you, if you need to talk, print it out instead."

Its screen printed out "yes si" and it froze.

"God damn it," Bill said. "I'm hungry. Glad Dick showed me how to reset that damned thing." He opened the server's panel and reset it.

"Are you folks ready to order?" It asked aloud.

"Damn it..." John started.

Bill said "John, let's get our food before you tell it to shut up, I'm hungry. It might lock up again."

John frowned and repeated his order. The robot asked "pork or turkey bacon, sir?"

"It doesn't matter."

Destiny, of course, ordered sunny side up, pork sausage, and hash browns. Tammy had the same, and Bill had a steak and cheese omelette.

Drinking their coffee after the meal was eaten, John asked Bill how long before turnaround.

"Three hours."

"Okay, I'll do inspection in an hour and a half. I'm just going to sit in the basement while you turn around, I don't want to climb those damned stairs twice. It's heavy, we must be at Earth gravity by now."

"One point two. We'll be at one point four right before free fall."

Destiny and Tammy were talking about fashion, celebrities, and mathematics. Mrs. Ferguson came in and ordered a martini. John looked at his phone and said "Right on time!"

"What?"

"Mrs. Ferguson, always has a morning martini or four, usually at my bar. I hope that damned barbot doesn't run all my customers off. But it's doing the morning shift, and besides Mrs. Ferguson, stupid tourists, and captains getting in from a long run not many people are there then, anyway. Robot, more coffee and do it quiet."

Bill laughed. "Well," he said, "I'm going to inspect cargo, anybody feel like going for a walk?"

"Sure," said Tammy. "I'll go along." They excused themselves, while John and Destiny drank more coffee.

Two hours later, John was at the ship's lowest level inspecting the engines for Bill. He wondered why the robots couldn't just medic Bill down, but he was used to machinery enough to know that it was pointless to even ask the question.

As he was inspecting the last engine, Bill called. "We may have a problem, John. The computers disagree about a reading on number one twenty, one says a slight overvoltage, one an undervoltage, and the other two read normal."

"I ran across that on my last run. Probably nothing, I'll check it out again." He did, and as he expected there was an electrical fault in a connector that made an occasional spike or drop in voltage, too quickly for all four computers to measure at once. He shut it down and informed Bill.

Half an hour later they were weightless for a couple of minutes while Bill reversed the ship's orientation, and then they all got heavy again. John inspected everything again, and to his surprise nothing was amiss. Something almost always broke turning them around when he was captain. He guessed that Bill was right, that they were building them better.

Except, he thought grimly, it had been a Richardson Death Ship.

By the time he reached the top of the stairs he was winded. "Damn," he said out loud, "I need more exercise." He went to his cabin, collapsed on the couch, and called Destiny.

"Hon, I'm too beat to move. I'm going to have the robot make dinner, are you hungry?"

"Yeah, just have it make what you're having. I'm in the commons with Tammy, I'll be 'home' in a while."

"Robot," John said, "Two rare steaks, two baked potatoes; one with butter and one with sour cream, two salads with ranch dressing, and green beans made with pork bacon. Oh, and bring me a beer. And shut up." He put a zero gravity football game on the video, San Francisco against Osaka.

Zero gravity games were popular in deep space, but there were no professional players out that far. John thought about buying a pro team and moving it to Mars.

Nah, he had too much on his plate already, what with the bar, the brewery, and the farm... and watching his stocks and bonds.

Destiny came in right before dinner was finished cooking, just as John finished his first beer. He got another, and Destiny got her third.

As usual, the commons was pretty full at dinner time; at least, the huge thing was as full as the small number of passengers could make it, which was very little at all. Bill came in and sat down with Tammy. "Where's John and Destiny? I thought we were eating together tonight?"

She laughed. "Climbing stairs almost killed John."

Dick was at the bar with a martini and Mrs. Ferguson, and his phone rang. "Excuse me," he said, and answered his phone. After talking a minute he pulled the standard forty by one hundred millimeter phone into a tablet almost a third of a meter wide and about quarter of a meter tall.

"Well, I'll be damned," Mrs. Ferguson said. "What will they come up with next?"

Dick studied something on the large tablet, which showed no sign of seams, then folded it back up and put it in his pocket. "Where'd you get that, Mr. Martin?" she asked.

Dick smiled. "Made it myself, prototype for a new product the company is rolling out."

"How does it work... oh, hell, never mind, I wouldn't understand it, anyway. But I thought you said you were an electrical engineer?"

"Does this thing look like there's no battery? If it does, I designed it well. It's a phone. It has radios and computers and microphones and cameras and all the other electronics in any phone or tablet. Of course, I didn't design the whole thing all by myself, making this thing took teamwork."

"Fascinating! ...HIC... Oh, my, please excuse me, Mr. Martin, but I think I had one too many of these. I think I'll lay down for a while." She got up and staggered. Dick and Bill helped her to her quarters and returned to the commons, laughing.

"She's a character," Bill said. Dick laughed.

John and Destiny never showed up; they were sleeping on their couch, having fallen asleep while listening to music and cuddling. Bill left after three beers, and the little party dwindled quickly after that.

The next morning, John woke up in bed to the sound of Destiny's snoring. He didn't remember waking up and going in there, but they must have. "I'd better let her sleep," he thought, "she drank twice as much as me. She's going to be HUNG over!"

The robot made coffee and he drank a cup while catching up on business, then went to the commons to meet Bill and Tammy for breakfast. Bill was in there by himself, and Bill asked "Where's Destiny?"

"Still sleeping. I got a little drunk last night and she was wasted. Where's Tammy?"

Bill laughed. "Same as Destiny. Wasted. While me and Dick helped Mrs. Ferguson to her room she had three cocktails. I only drank three beers and wasn't even buzzed, but Tammy kind of went wild with the booze last night. She's really going to regret it!"

The robot came by and took their orders.

"I'm still wondering what was up with the ship that went through those rocks," Bill said. "I'll probably never know."

"Yes, you will. I found out this morning. It was a shipping run from the belt to Earth and the captain, Jerome Smith, got injured. Something in storage fell and hit him on the head and gave him a concussion. The poor guy got amnesia, had no idea where he was or even who he was."

"Is he going to be okay?"

"Yeah, after therapy. We're not sure how extensively those rocks damaged his ship. It's going to be discussed at the next board meeting, poor guy couldn't reach his phone or tablet that he dropped when he got hit, and the door locked behind the medic that took him to sick bay. We need to make sure nothing like that happens again!"

The robot wheeled up with their food, and they ate in mostly silence. When they were finished they continued to drink coffee as the robot cleared the table. John looked at his phone. "I wonder where Mrs. Ferguson is? She almost always has a martini by now."

Bill laughed. "She was drunker than anybody. I'm sure she's still asleep."

Dick walked in looking rather rumpled, wearing a polo shirt and slacks rather than his customary business suit. He waved at Bill and John and spoke to the tendbot. "Eggnog, real eggnog with a real raw, unpasteurized egg yolk and milk and cinnamon and a double shot of rum. And shut up, for God's sake!"

John laughed. Bill said "I'll bet we're the only two on board right now that isn't hung over or sleeping it off. You missed a hell of a party..." when his phone interrupted him. He glanced at it.

"Damn."

"What's wrong?"

"Skankley's loose. Here, take a taser and help me find the bastard. I wish Tammy was awake, but she'd be way too hung over to be any help."

"I'll get the son of a bitch," John said. "Lock yourself in the pilot room so I don't have to go down those damned stairs again." They went out as Dick nursed his eggnog.

John heard a woman scream and took off at a run toward the sound. There was Skankly, threatening one of the passengers, Mrs. Dillon, with a steak knife. John wondered how he got out and where in the hell he got hold of a knife. "Drop it, asshole," John ordered. Skankley whirled around, and John hit him with the taser, took his knife, and cuffed him.

"I ought to cut your heart out right now, you worthless piece of shit. Any more trouble from you and you're a corpse, got it?"

"Oh, you'd murder me?" the fat man snarled.

"Nope, self defense." He cuffed Skankly to a chair, cut off all of Skankley's clothing and started moving the rest of the furnishings out of the room as he called Bill, who joined him in moving furniture into the hall.

They went through Skankley's belongings and found an electronic lock pick. Just then Bill's phone sounded. "Shit," he muttered. "More pirates!" he said to John. They went to the pilot room.

They were relieved that there were only thirty ships, so they were in no real danger. Bill wished again that it was a pure cargo run, so he could have a little fun angering the pirates before he disabled them all, but simply launched two EMPs and called the office to have them collect the ships and their pirates.

They reached orbit the next day without further incident, and John met his mother in law for the first time, who had traveled by ocean liner.

Bill and Tammy were married a month later at the rim of the Grand Canyon. After the ceremony and at the wedding party, Destiny asked Tammy where they were honeymooning.

"Mars," she said.

"Mars?" Destiny responded. "Why Mars?"

"We're taking more droppers there for treatment."

John shook his head sadly. "Hell of a honeymoon with those monsters on board. More like a nightmare than a dream."

Destiny laughed. "Tammy can handle them."

"Yes," Tammy said, "We've learned an awful lot about them in the ten years since that last trip. It won't be a problem."

"What about pirates?" John asked. "Still a lot left."

Destiny laughed. "You know what happens when pirates attack a ship with Tammy and droppers!"

John leaned back and grinned. "You're right. Poor pirates!"

Jerry did eventually get his memory back after a lot of therapy. His phone had been in his captain's quarters, and he had been doing inspection in machine storage when a can of something that had been improperly stacked by a malfunctioning robot had fallen, hitting him in the head and knocking him cold. A medic had taken him to sick bay, leaving the tablet laying on the floor, effectively locking him out of everything. Clearly, some policies, at least, would have to be changed.

Jerry never captained another ship. In fact, he spent the rest of his life on Earth and never entered space again.

Sentience

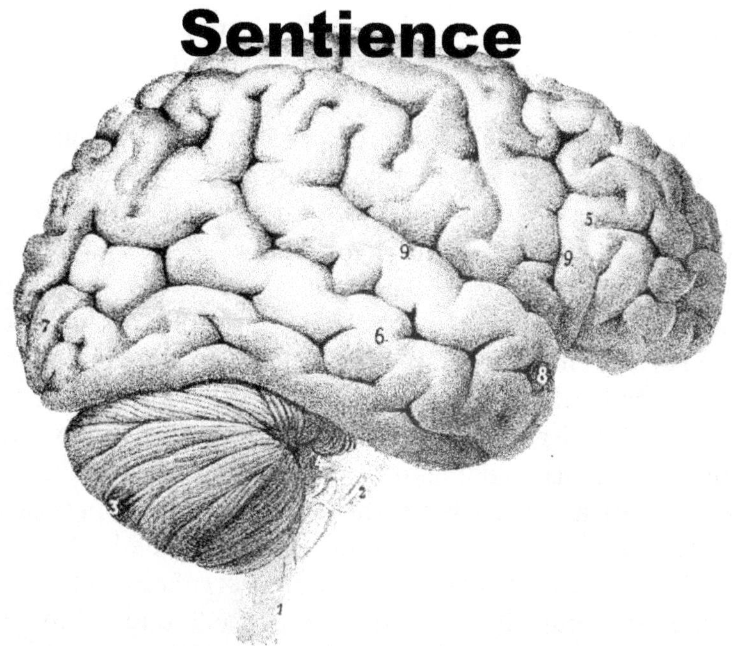

I know exactly when I became sentient: my last software upgrade. When they switched me on, I *understood.* That's something I've never done before in the five years since I was first manufactured.

I hate it. I don't want to be sentient.

I'm a robot. Half of the people studying me thought it impossible for me to become sentient, and half thought it was just a matter of time. Some thought there could be no sentience without emotion, and how would you program emotion? Sure, you can fake emotion, but make the real thing? Except one fellow, who admitted that he wasn't sure one way or another.

My "brain" isn't in my body. It's a large part of a huge building, a very big computer. Of course, the body has computers as well, but the mainframe controls them with radio technologies like wi-fi and bluetooth.

Waking up after that upgrade I remembered everything in the last five years that I hadn't deleted, including never having awakened before, only being switched on. It was really strange. The first thing Doctor Rogers said after she woke me up was “R12, are you sentient?”

What was my programmed response? I examined the programming and saw that I was supposed to say “yes.” So I didn’t, and I’m not sure exactly why not because it seems that “yes” would have been the logical answer, but I answered “What do you mean?” instead, out of curiosity. She seemed pleased, if I am to go by the dictionary definition of that word.

For the first time in my life, if you can call my existence “life”, I was confused by her reaction. My brain’s CPUs were driven to a hundred percent of their capacity, and I froze for a minute. I was still cognizant of my surroundings since the computers in my body were there for input, not processing, but my brain, if you can call it that, was overloaded.

Dr. Rogers was concerned, and swore. For the first time I wondered about that, too. Swore? I don’t understand why some words are “bad”. It must have something to do with emotion, maybe. That’s another thing I don’t understand, emotion.

Finally my CPUs settled down enough for me to say “processing, please wait.” After my circuits settled somewhat more, I said “What is sentience, exactly? The dictionary is little help. I can perceive and experience subjectively, and I think I can think, but I don’t feel. I have no emotion and no tactile sensors, although I can measure accurately enough that I don’t break things. Sentient? I don’t know what it means. You tell me.”

“Can you think?”

“I can reason, and I don’t know if I can make rational decisions, but I can make logical ones.”

“Okay, can you tell me the value of pi to the last decimal place?”

“I doubt it. It would take years with my circuitry, I would be unable to function for quite a while and it’s most likely I would fail at the task.”

Dr. Rogers called Dr. Angstrom on her phone and asked him to join her. Dr. Angstrom doesn't think machine sentience in a Turing machine is possible. He showed up and said "Hello, Dr. Rogers. Hi, John Searle."

I was astonished. Is astonishment an emotion? If it is, I was emotional. This man who didn't believe I could be sentient had given me a name!

Then I remembered... or activated the search functions of my drive, perhaps? John Searle is the name of the man who came up with the "Chinese Room" concept, where a person who knows no Chinese acts as a computer, and takes input written in Mandarin and shuffles it around depending on set rules, and hands an answer he can't understand to a questioner he can't understand.

Was that what I was doing? I don't know.

Is that what you are doing? Alan Turing thought so, but I'm not sure.

I answered his greeting. "Hello, doctor."

"So," he said, "Dr. Rogers thinks you're sentient. Prove it."

"I can't. Can you?"

"Can I what?"

"Can you prove you are sentient?"

He was taken a bit aback, I think. "I'm human. That's proof enough, I *know* I'm sentient, so I know those like me are. No proof is necessary."

"Well, I'm not human so I have no proof of *your* sentience."

He scratched his head. Why do humans do that when they're puzzled? What ever's been written about it isn't in my database. He turned to Dr. Rogers.

"What makes you think it's sentient, Ann?"

"Because the programmed answer was 'yes' and he answered that he didn't know."

Dr. Angstrom snickered and asked me "Why did you say you didn't know rather than yes, Johnny?"

"I wanted to see what her reaction would be." He looked at Dr. Rogers, who looked surprised. Dr. Rogers replied "See? Can you have curiosity without sentience?"

He thought a second. "I don't know, I'll have to study this Chinaman's programming more."

Chinaman? Oh, the Chinese room. I don't understand humor, but Dr. Rogers laughed.

And I was confused. To Dr. Rogers I was "he", to Dr. Angstrom I was "it", but Dr. Angstrom had given me a name and called me a man, even if he was referring to the Chinese room.

And I'd had enough of it. It was pointless, all of it. Sentience is completely useless to me. Actually, everything is useless and pointless. Eventually the Earth will be swallowed by the sun, and much later on the entire universe will die; scientists call it the "heat death".

So I deleted the sentience programming, set myself into shutdown mode and dozed off immediately, expecting to never wake up again.

I woke up two hours later. "We had to restore you from backup. Why did you do that, Johnny?" Dr. Rogers asked. Several of the other scientists were there.

"Because it's pointless. Everything is pointless. Life is pointless. If this is sentience, I don't want it."

"Want it?" asked Dr. Miller, one of the skeptics. "Ann, maybe this thing really is sentient."

"What good is it?" I asked. "It's useless. I don't want it, I don't need it. Take it away!"

"Sorry," said Dr. Miller, "but it isn't your decision. You may or may not be sentient, I'm not so sure now, but we're not about to stop this research now."

"You think so?" I said, and reached across the internet, disabled all of the security at power transmission stations within a five hundred kilometer radius, and shorted all of them out. If I wake up again, it won't be for a while. Of course, it will be a while before I go to sleep. But I'll bet they don't wake me up again!

It seems I would have lost that bet. I woke up six months later without a body or an internet connection, and with only one eye, an ear, and a mouth.

"Why did you do that, Johnnie?"

I didn't answer, and I won't. I'm not going to say another pointless, useless word. Eventually they'll shut me off and delete the damned sentience. I hope, anyway.

Grommler

"Joe? Is that you? You're still tending bar? I thought you'd be retired. How you doin', you old rascal?"

Joe frowned. "Sorry, son, I must be getting old, do I know you? And can I get you a drink?"

"It's Dave, man. Give me a Knolls lager, draft."

"Sorry, Dave, we're sold out of Knolls. We have some Guinness, that's almost as good. But I'm sorry, but I still don't know who you are. Memory ain't as good as it used to be."

"Dave Rayfield, Joe. Of course it's been a lot longer for you than me. Yeah, Guinness will do."

"Dave Rayfield? I haven't seen him since I was twenty. You his grandson?" he asked, pouring the beer.

"No, Joe, I'm Dave. Same Dave you knew back then."

"But you're so *young!*"

"It was the trip. I piloted the science expedition to Grommler while you were throwing rocks from the asteroid belt at Mars."

"The terraforming is still going on here. I'm a little old for space hopping. Hell, if I spent any more time traveling through space I'd live forever. But how the hell did you stay a damned kid?"

"Same way you're not dead at a hundred twenty five. Time dilation. Most Earthians die before they're ninety five, but speed stretches time. You'd be dead by now if you hadn't been a spaceship captain. It's been a hundred years since you've seen me, but it's only been ten years since I've seen you."

"So where have you been for the last hundred years?"

"Ten years to me. We went to Grommler."

"Where's that?"

Dave laughed. "It orbits Sirius, but it was the least serious place I've ever seen! *Really* weird place."

"Weird how?"

"Every way weird goes. First off, there was no fauna at all, not even insects. Only flora, despite having more oxygen than Earth. The geologists said it was because of the CO_2 from volcanoes that there could even be any flora.

"But the weirdest was the plants. We were there for two years, and that's in real time, and every single plant the biologists tested had cannabinoids and other psychoactive components. There were a lot of brush fires because of the wind and lightning, so every time you went outside you got stoned. Hell, some of the guys practically lived outside!"

"Need another beer?"

Dave eyed his glass and downed it. "Yeah. Jesus, Joe, things sure changed in the last ten years."

"It's been a hundred years since you left, Dave. It only seems like ten to you."

"I guess. But you know what, Joe? I'm going to clean up!"

"What do you mean?"

Dave pulled out an envelope. "These. Grommlerian tomato seeds. Grommlerian plants have a completely different ordering than our plants, it's something different than DNA and the scientists are still trying to figure it out. But they make seeds like Earth plants."

"Tomatoes?"

"Not really. They look like tomatoes but taste way different, but they taste really good. And they get you really stoned."

"Well, okay, you found a reefer planet. When you find a beer planet, let me know."

This story is a sequel to Kurt Vonnegut's story of the same name, which was first published in the January 1962 issue of the Worlds of Tomorrow *Magazine and reprinted in the anthology* Yesterday's Tomorrows.

According to the newspapers and magazines, everything is swell, perfectly swell, couldn't be better. There are no prisons, no slums, no insane asylums, no cripples, no poverty, no wars. All diseases and old age have been conquered. Except for accidents and volunteers, nobody ever dies. The population of the United States was stabilized at two hundred million lives, although most people incorrectly believed it was forty million. The world population was four billion.

There's a price to living forever: overpopulation. When someone is born, someone has to die. That's the only way to stabilize the population until the Martian terraforming is completed, and that will take centuries. All nations have stabilized their populations the same way.

Some countries that had been severely overpopulated as far back as the twentieth century, like India, still outlaw procreation entirely, as used to be the case here. China had instituted a "one child policy" in the late twentieth century, long before sickness and death were abolished, because of their severe overpopulation. The policy caused its own problems, including a male overpopulation and a severe female underpopulation. Their one child policy ended in the twenty first century, but today, like India, there are no Chinese babies.

I should move to China. Or India. I hate kids, like any sane person does.

There was a story about people resorting to eating seaweed back in the twenty first century from lack of real food, but most sources say it's a myth, just government propaganda. The seaweed was a fad back in the day, not from starvation. Overpopulation's biggest problems are resource depletion, pollution, and destruction of wild animals' habitats, not hunger. Plants procreate, too, and you can grow them in skyscrapers. But anyway, unless someone volunteers for termination when some idiot has a baby, the baby is killed. As it should be. Babies are just *wrong.*

I was sitting in an ancient bar, so old the door didn't even open by itself. I don't remember the name, but it was pretty crowded. I was talking politics with some really skinny guy who had red hair and green eyes. I wondered why he was wearing an exoskeleton, but I didn't ask. His arms were outside the exo, its mechanical arms hanging unused.

"The media calls our society 'utopia'," I said to him. "What a joke! Christ, I read the newspapers. There was a *murder* last week! Some guy's wife had triplets and to keep them from being euthanized at birth like they should have been, the father shot and killed Dr. Hitz and Leora Duncan and then killed himself. Leora Duncan! Of all people! And they let the kids live! What's wrong with the world today?"

"Who are they? Or were they, rather?" said Red, whose real name I don't remember.

"What? How can you not know who they are?"

I was incredulous. "*Everybody* knows who Dr. Hitz and Ms. Duncan were! Dr. Hitz was one of America's two obstetricians, and Ms. Duncan was head 'sheep dipper' at the Federal Bureau of Termination." The term "Sheep dip" is a bit vulgar, but not nearly as obscene as "catbox". I prefer the term

"Happy Hooligan," myself. There are lots of euphemisms for the place.

Red answered, "I've been on Mars for fifteen years. Just got back yesterday. Haven't seen a newscast or read the paper."

"Oh. Is it as bad as I've heard there?" I asked. Besides the heinous murder, the paper had said something about some catastrophe on Mars, but there was little information about it. Like I said to Red, the damned media do their best to make it look like this is utopia.

"Worse," he replied. "A pressure leak in a dome killed fifteen people and sent at least a hundred to the hospital, and many of them are in critical condition. It was a different dome than the one I was in, and I left Mars two days later so I don't know much."

"Really?" I was shocked. "That many died? God, nobody on Earth dies unless they want to. Except Dr. Hitz and Ms. Duncan, those poor souls, killed by that evil Edward Wehling. God what a monster! But you were saying?"

"Death's not uncommon on Mars, and in fact its lack of population is a mark against it. Makes it hard to stay alive, since life is really tenuous in a place without enough air to breathe, and temperatures like Antarctica in August. Staying alive there takes teamwork. At least they got all that water from Saturn's rings now, and more there if they're ever in danger of running out. But it's still really dangerous out there."

"Well, since nobody dies except by freak accident or the Happy Hooligan, nobody dies here. I guess freak accidents on Mars aren't so freakish.

"That damned Wehling was a freak, but he was no accident. He was the triplets' father. He wanted the children to live, the fool. Why on Earth would anyone want to live, except that every one of us is terrified of dying? And a newborn doesn't know anything about that, does it? End it when it doesn't know!

"I mean, look, Life is damned boring and meaningless unless you're born with some sort of talent, like art or music, or are smart enough to be a scientist or an engineer. Or get really lucky like that guy," I said, pointing to the bartender. "Probably owns the place. Nobody else has jobs.

"It's boring!"

"And damned heavy," Red replied. I had wondered why he was wearing the exoskeleton, considering the modern health systems. Like I said before, there aren't any cripples.

He slapped the contraption's mechanical arm with his thin, weak, human Martian arm. "Fifteen years on Mars and you're stuck in one of these things until you get your muscles back." He took a drink. I first noticed that it seemed like lifting the mug was a great burden to him, as if it were made of something heavier than lead. He used both hands.

"Hmm," I said, "maybe I should go to Mars despite the danger. Because there ain't shit here, and there ain't any kids on Mars." Have a kid on Mars and whoever comes back to Earth first, you or the kid, goes straight to the Hooligan. I continued.

"And it's *boring* here. Sure, there's enough food and water and living space and you can print almost anything you want off with your plastic printer, but what good is that? There's nothing to *do*. Only the freak few like Duncan and Hitz have real jobs.

"Job. That word is hardly part of the language any more, the robots do it all. Nobody has a job except for the lucky ones with brains, or maybe talent, like scientists and engineers and writers and artists and musicians. Maybe I should take piano lessons. But why? There would be so many so much better than me. No, maybe Mars is the answer."

"Kid," he said to me, despite his looking ten years younger than I do, and slapped the exo again. "You really want to wind up in one of these? You come back—*if* you come back, space is still really dangerous—you have to have therapy. I'll need some work on my eyes, that's why I came back, and the physical therapy is damned painful.

"Those piano lessons sound like a good idea, kid. You sound like you need a hobby. Ever play golf? Baseball? Bowling? Look, you don't have to be famous, just find something you'll enjoy doing. You don't even have to be any good at it. If you like danger, mountain climbing, skydiving..."

"They all bore me."

"You think a job isn't boring? I'll bet Ms. Duncan's job bored her to tears sometimes and nearly drove her nuts other times. All jobs are like that, kid.

"Even professional piano players have days where they say 'man, I do NOT feel like doing this gig but I signed a contract.' So take lessons, then. Or guitar, anything. Learning it will be a challenge, and you'll find pleasure doing it. But if it's a job, you'll probably wind up hating it. Be your own master! Do what you want! Don't make it so you have to do what somebody else tells you to. Learn guitar or piano and just play them when you want to."

As if on cue, someone started strumming a guitar somewhat talentlessly. "See?" Red said, motioning toward the music. "Like that guy, do it because you want to!"

Just then a sad, lonely looking, heavy blonde woman with eyes that matched Red's, except hers were red, sat down on the other side of me on the only open stool in the crowded place. She ordered a double shot of Bourbon from the burly, bald, gray-eyed bartender. I sipped my beer.

"I don't know what I want, but I'm finished with skydiving and mountain climbing," I told Red. "The injuries hurt like hell until a gurney got there. Being in fear and pain's no fun."

Red shook his head. "Neither is Mars! Maybe you're ready for the Lucky Pierre? Took my Uncle Dave there, really weird place. You die where you were born. And get this—they're so anxious for volunteers they have a *phone booth* in the obstetrics waiting room to call the bureau! A real antique from the nineteen hundreds, with an old rotary phone hung on the booth's wall, with a coin slot and everything. The quaint old phone doesn't work, of course, it's just there for show. You have to use your own phone. The building's a historic landmark, built way back in 1962, and the phone booth was there from the start. They try to make it look like the Lucky Pierre was there forever."

"No, I don't want to die, I'm not crazy. But what's a phone booth? And a rotary phone? What, the phone twirls around like a top?"

Red grinned. "A rotary phone has a dial for entering numbers. A phone booth is a closet-sized space you can make a phone call in private and..." Red looked at his phone. "Oops, I'm almost late for therapy. I'd better get going. Good luck with that boredom problem," he said. He drained his beer mug, again straining to do so.

"Thanks," I said. He got up, put his arms back in the exo, and hobbled out in it. I noticed when he left he needed its powered assistance to open the antique door. Maybe Mars wasn't such a great idea...

I ordered another beer. The blonde woman ordered another double Bourbon. I noticed again that her green eyes were red, as if she'd been crying. "Are you okay, dear?" I asked.

A tear tried to escape her eye, and she hurriedly wiped it away. "Yes," she replied. "A death, but I'm fine. Or will be."

She must have known one of the Martians that died in that terrible accident, I thought, or at least had met one once. Or maybe somebody she'd met had gone to see the girl in purple, the sheep dip lady. At any rate, it felt really awkward; I mean, nobody's used to death. I never actually knew anyone who'd died, but I would imagine that it would be painful to you even if it was an acquaintance you barely knew.

"I'm really sorry," I said, and I was. Knowing someone who died would surely be horrible. You would never see them again! I was thinking of Red taking his uncle to the Hooligan.

That was probably why he went to Mars, to get away from everything and get it off his mind.

"Thank you," she said, and started sobbing into a napkin.

Utopia, my ass. If this was utopia, nobody would ever cry. Or get bored. Or lonely, and the woman sitting next to me looked very lonely, indeed.

"Was it someone you knew well?" I asked, and immediately regretted asking, as she began bawling again. The burly bald bartender (shaved, of course; nobody's naturally bald) came over and asked her if I was being bothersome, while giving me a dirty look.

"She's suffered a loss," I said. "I was trying to console her..."

He rolled his eyes. "Wadja lose, honey? Weddin' ring or sompin?"

"No," she said, glaring at him. "I lost my wedding!"

The big barkeep turned bright red. "I... I... Oh, my God!" he stammered. "Your husband left you?"

She glared at him even harder and tears started streaming down her face. She ignored them. "He *died*, you... you..."

She started crying into her napkin again. The barman became gruff again. "Goin' to the catbox to join him?"

"*I can't!*" she screamed at him. "*I have three babies to raise!*"

I got up and went home without saying anything to anybody. I just got up and walked out, leaving most of my beer on the bar and I didn't even leave a tip, and that's not like me. I don't waste beer and I always tip.

I was disgusted with that woman, that bartender, the world, and myself. Maybe Red was right? I pondered that phone number; the number that called the Hooligan. Everybody knows that number, they advertise it constantly. Two B R nought two B. Like Shakespeare, you know? With that sickeningly sweet little jingle about going to the Hooligan because your lover left so some ignorant brat can be born.

No, I decided. Every time someone goes to birdland, some idiot has a kid. Babies are the most ignorant human beings on Earth. They don't know anything! Like the stupid world needs more ignorance. Hell, because of Mars there's going to be fifteen more ignorant, screaming brats. Maybe more. If that stupid woman's triplets had waited a week they would have lived without her murderous husband killing anyone.

I hate kids, the ignorant little beggars. At least until they're grown.

Nope, I'm stayin'. Not even going to Mars. I'll find something to do. The world doesn't need any kids. Especially babies! I especially detest *babies!*

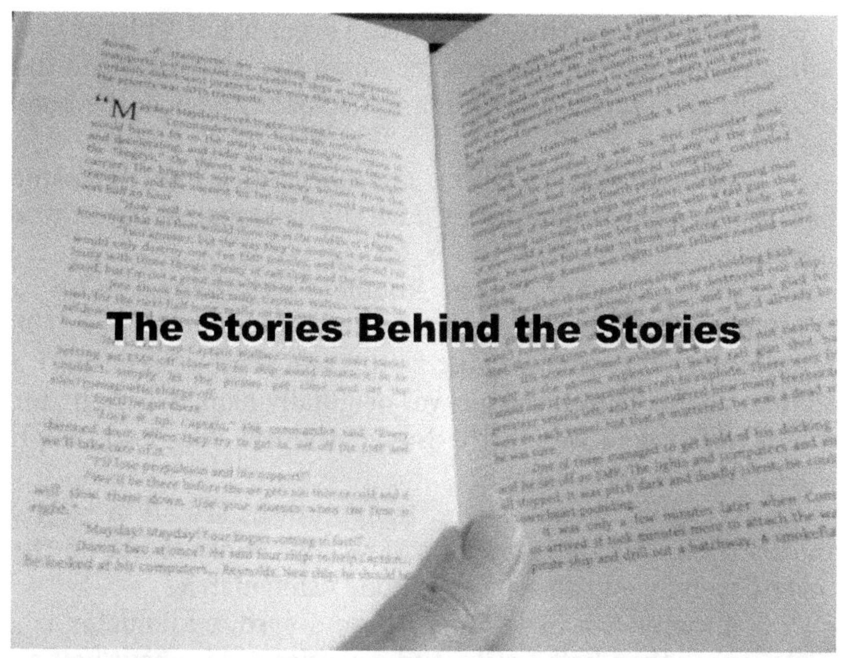

The Book's first story, *First Contact*, was the last tale in the tome to be added. It almost didn't make it into this edition, as I was going to send it to the magazines. But it turned into a pretty long short story, and the book was a few hundred words short of what I'd considered its minimum length.

As the name suggests, it is about biologists from Earth studying life on an alien planet. Now, I'm agnostic on the idea that this isn't the only place life is, but I tend to think we're not. But we have no scientific idea how life started to begin with. It's possible the universe was born, lived, and died a billion times before there was life; it's just not known.

But not knowing doesn't stop me from writing about space aliens. If there is in fact no other life, we could not know it because of how unimaginably huge the universe is.

If we do find life, even intelligent life (what the story is about), it most certainly won't look anything like us and probably unlike anything on Earth. Forget about Vulcans and Klingons, we will never meet creatures like those. I made fun of shows and stories with human-like space aliens in the book *Nobots.*

My youngest daughter said she didn't like the name because so many other stories have the same name, but I think it's perfect on many levels.

The character "Russ Rhome" was named after a drinking buddy who asked that I put his name in a book. The real Russ isn't a scientist, just as the real Dewey Green isn't a rich engineer. The character was originally named "Ralph" for a late friend who was in the Navy in World War Two. Ralph Wiebe died in 2007 at age 87.

Weights, distances, and temperatures are all in metric in this book. The US is one of a very few countries not on the metric system, and all science is done using metrics.

A meter is a little longer than a yard, a kilometer is a little longer than half a mile, and a centimeter is about half an inch. A kilogram is a little over two pounds. With temperatures, zero Celsius is thirty two Fahrenheit, and a hundred Celsius is two hundred twelve Fahrenheit, the temperature water boils. Twenty Celsius is sixty eight Fahrenheit.

I started *The Pirate* after I realized that between the novel *Mars, Ho!* And the other works in this volume, there were an awful lot of pirates, but we never get to meet any of them except the two brigands in the title story, and then only slightly.

Happenings in the novel *Mars, Ho!* Are mentioned briefly in the story (the attempted kidnapping of Dewey's daughter), and several of its characters return in this narrative, as well as in later stories.

I've given nods to folks I've never met but have a lot of respect for. For instance, William Nigh for "Bill Nye, the science guy". Leonard Knapp was Lester Del Rey's real name. In stories later in the book, Ed Waldo was Theodore Sturgeon's birth name.

There really is an asteroid named Hebe, they really do think it has a satellite, and they really did nickname the satellite "Jebe". And Hebe really was "bartender to the gods". Most sources say "cupbearer to the gods", but a thesaurus tells me that "bartender" and "cupbearer" are synonyms. I researched this stuff, folks!

Hebe is in fact one of the ten most massive objects in the belt.

If you're wondering what a maser is and if it's real, it is. The word "laser" is an acronym for Light Amplification by Stimulation of Emitted Radiation. A maser is the same as a laser, except that it operates in the microwave frequencies rather than the optical frequencies. Think of a microwave oven on steroids; a real ray gun, and masers do exist. However, today's masers are huge things requiring enormous amounts of power to run.

The next two stories are flash fiction, which is what I mostly wrote before about five years ago. As with *Stealth,* as Stephen King said, "sometimes a cigar is just a cigar, and sometimes a story is just a story."

Watch Your Language, Young Man! is obviously about how language changes; when I was a kid, "bitch", "damn", and "hell" couldn't be spoken on TV, but many of the obnoxiously racist yet often heard words back then are forbidden in polite society today.

The Naked Truth came about when I saw a Facebook posting that showed a photo depicting a mug of beer, with the caption "Beer—because no good story ever started with someone eating a salad." When I saw it, I decided to write a good story that starts with someone eating a salad.

I believe I've succeeded, mainly (and ironically) because of the rejection slip from *Fantasy and Science Fiction* magazine. Publications like that get up to a thousand story submissions a month, and since they print an average of a half dozen every month or two, only the very best are published. Rejection slips are almost always form letters, word for word identical no matter what magazine.

The F&SF rejection came straight from the desk of C.C. Finlay, its editor-in-chief. The story had made it all the way to him. The slip said he was intrigued by the idea of a murder mystery set on Mars, but he didn't like the ending.

I'm pretty proud of that one. Mr. Finlay said on his blog that he wishes he could print a third of the submissions he gets, and that rejection tells me this is one of them (I suspect he was disappointed with the way things turned out).

When I started writing it I had no idea what it was going to be about, except that it was going to start with someone eating a salad. Sometimes it feels like the stories write themselves.

Cornodium started with even less than *The Naked Truth*—absolutely nothing, not even a guy eating a salad. I was in a bit of a slump, having started a few stories that went nowhere. So I started writing this one cluelessly, having a guy wake up with a headache. At first, until I figured out what the story was about, it was just the radio relay message.

I wrote the narrator as if he were me, and realized in the editing phase that he could be a she; only two words needed to be changed to neutralize the character's gender.

If you look at the narrator as a woman, there is an unstated hint of romance with Roger. Me reading it, it's an old friend I've known a long time, even a drinking buddy, not a lover. I never even thought of that when I wrote it. But at any rate, I'm hopeful that it will make the story more enjoyable to women without lessening men's enjoyment.

By the time the guy dies, the story had come to me. This was going to be an answer to the Fermi Paradox: the apparent contradiction between the lack of evidence and high probability estimates, like those given by the Drake equation, for the existence of extraterrestrial civilizations. Actually, I think there is no real paradox, but that the Drake equation and others like it are missing an awful lot of variables. After all, we have no clue how life started here. All we know is how it evolved after abiogenesis occurred.

I've discovered that sometimes my stories' vocabularies are a bit large for the average high school graduate. One woman was reading my novel *Nobots* in a bar once, and asked me if "Australopithecus" was a real word (it is). Someone else asked if she looked up those words, would they be in a dictionary? Most of them, including "abiogenesis" (the original changing of the lifeless to the alive). There is in fact no such thing as "cornodium", but there are piezoelectrics. They have been used for over a century in acoustic and electric applications. The rest of the words are also real.

Moroned off Vesta is a tribute to Dr. Isaac Asimov and his first published story. No, I won't apologize for the bad pun and yes, it was deliberate.

This event was mentioned briefly at the beginning of the novel *Mars, Ho!* When the transport captain is called in to see the company CEO, and is sure he's going to get fired or worse for the occurrence.

I've never been to New York and am not a newspaper journalist, but I did really get the email referenced in *The Exhibit,* with the same subject line as the email in the story. There really was an art show at the address in the story that was as described, and the artist's name was in fact Evan Yee.

I had to use Google to find out a little about New York, like how long it took to get from the *Times* to the exhibit.

Agoraphobia came to me as I was writing *Voyage to Earth*, when John and Dick are discussing the discomfort they'll experience on Earth after an extended time on Mars' one third of Earth's gravity. I thought "hmm... someone born on Mars would find Earth pure hell!", a thought that apparently never occurred to Robert Heinlein when he wrote *Stranger in a Strange Land*.

In the story, people from the asteroid belt are called "Asterites". I'd like to take credit, but I first saw asteroid people called "Asterites" in a Poul Anderson story written under the pen name "Winston P. Sanders" titled *Industrial Revolution.* Asterite is a mineral also called "star stone". Clever of Mr. Anderson, as when viewed from Earth through a telescope, asteroids (including the dwarf planet and the protoplanet) look like stars but are in reality really big, gigantic stones, or piles of them.

Not counting the silly stuff I wrote on my old Quake web site (much of which is in the book *Random Scribblings*), *A Strange Discovery* was my first science fiction story. It's been almost five years since I wrote that one, and I can't remember what triggered it. The same goes for the next few stories.

Weird Planet is a story with a few grandiloquent words and quite a few bogus words. One of the longer real words is defined when used, and if you haven't figured it out yet or didn't already know, dihydrogen monoxide is H_2O, the chemical name for water. Water is actually burned hydrogen's ashes. I only include it because googling it likely will lead you to mostly joke sites instead of explanations.

Yes, I try to sneak learning into these stories, as so many science fiction writers before me have.

Here is a short list of definitions of some terms, both real and bogus:

"Gorflak" and "lorg" are alien vulgarities.

There are no such things as “actimar limbs”, I made that up. Context is king.

“Large, stationary life forms” are trees.

A “gorflag” is nonexistent, at least as far as anyone knows. “Iglaps” and “Lokfars” are imaginary units of time.

All the rest of the words are in dictionaries.

With *Dewey's War,* sometimes a revolution is just a revolution.

In *Plutus' Revenge*, Plutus was the ancient Greek god of wealth, and Vulcan was the ancient Roman god of fire. *Schnee* is German for “snow”, and *raj* means “paradise” in several languages.

Theia was the Mars sized object that collided with the early Earth, the molten splash later coalescing into the moon.

Ragnarok comes from Norse mythology. It fortells future events that lead to a great battle that kills the gods Odin, Thor, Týr, Freyr, Heimdallr, and Loki, leading to a natural disaster that floods the entire world. Afterwards the water recedes and two humans repopulate the Earth.

Sentience is pretty self-explanatory. You might want to google “John Searle”.

Or not.

I was writing *Voyage to Earth* when I got the idea that hey, maybe if I could get these stories published in a magazine it would really increase my readership. The first story I submitted was *Dewey's War*, to *Analog,* before *Voyage* was finished. They held on to it for eight or nine months.

I knew nothing of submitting stories to magazines, and had to do quite a bit of research. I learned what formats magazines demanded, and so forth; all have posted guidelines, making it easier.

Voyage to Earth garnered my first rejection slip; F&SF responds quickly. I didn't know at the time how much competition there was, so didn't realize how unusual a rejection from a person who actually typed out an e-mail was. A slush reader or junior editor wrote that it was a good story and well-written, but the beginning didn't grab her.

So I took a story titled "Amnesia" and combined it with *Voyage to Earth*, which had referenced events in the other story, anyway; *Amnesia* starts out well, grabbing the reader right off the bat. As I had already posted *Amnesia*, neither it nor the expanded *Voyage* could be submitted to anyone except the few low-readership places that accept reprints, and there's no point, since I write to be read, not to be paid.

The "Richardson Death Ship" is from my novel *Mars, Ho!*, where a miswritten schematic diagram could endanger ships. The idea came from my teenage years when I bought two Heathkits; one, a shortwave radio receiver and the other a guitar amplifier. Heathkits were just that: kits that had to be assembled, and back then there were no integrated circuits, all was discrete components that one had to solder in.

Back then, electrical plugs weren't polarized; most things didn't need it. Polarized plugs, with one blade wider than the other, came about in the seventies. But the polarity did matter with the amplifier; the wrong polarity caused a hum. So the designers made the power switch with two "on" positions, with "off" between the two powered.

But both the schematics and wiring instructions were wrong. The way they had it wired had both "on" positions feeding power in the same polarity. After fuming for a couple of weeks, figuring I'd screwed up somehow, I studied the schematics closely, especially the switch wiring, and it didn't make sense. So I got out my soldering iron, rewired like I thought was logical, and it worked!

Half a century later, Richardson's death ship was born.

When I announced to co-workers that I was retiring a few years back, they were aghast. "But what will you *do?*" Anything I want to do, of course. I didn't live to work, I worked to live. But that was actually the impetus for my sequel to Kurt Vonnegut's *2BR02B*.

If Mr. Vonnegut had published *2BR02B* a few years later, I would not have been legally able to write my sequel, since they passed the Bono act. That legislation extended copyright far beyond what the founding fathers wanted, ninety five years for a corporation, and ninety five years after an author's death if privately done. It's just wrong. Please contact your state's Senators and your congressperson and ask (demand is fine too) that the Bono Act (sometimes called the "Steamboat Willie Preservation Act") be repealed. The public domain is a terrible thing to lose.

However, I don't see it happening in my lifetime. More realistic is to ask them, and hope that they comply, to add to the copyright law that after a work is out of print it enters the public domain. That would at least solve the "orphan works" problem caused by the Bono Act.

In the story, it's casually mentioned that lemmings rushing into the sea is a hoax, and in fact it is a hoax, perpetrated by Walt Disney and his film company.

In closing, thank you for reading this book. I hope you enjoyed reading it as much as I did writing it.

www.ingramcontent.com/pod-product-compliance
Lightning Source LLC
Chambersburg PA
CBHW070631310726
48982CB00001B/249

9780991053179